Hillhead Library
348 Byres Road
Glasgow G12 8AP
Phone: 0141 276 1617 Fax 276 1618

This book is due for return on or before the last date shown below. It may be renewed by telephone, personal application, fax or post, quoting this date, author, title and the book number

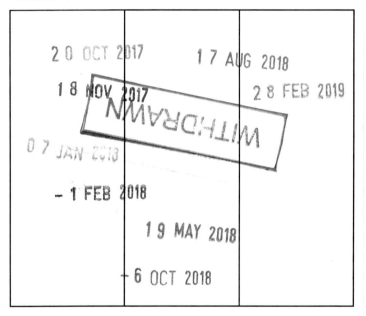

Glasgow Life and its service brands, including Glasgow Libraries, (found at www.glasgowlife.org.uk) are operating names for Culture and Sport Glasgow

Glasgow
CITY COUNCIL

Friend of My Youth

AMIT CHAUDHURI

Friend of My Youth

FABER & FABER

First published in 2017
by Faber & Faber Limited
Bloomsbury House
74–77 Great Russell Street
London WC1B 3DA

Typeset by Faber & Faber Limited
Printed and bound in the UK by CPI Group (UK) Ltd, Croydon, CRO 4YY

A CIP record for this book
is available from the British Library

ISBN 978-0-571-33759-0

2 4 6 8 10 9 7 5 3 1

In loving memory of my mother,
Bijoya Chaudhuri

FRIEND OF MY YOUTH

'We have long forgotten the ritual by which the house of our life was erected. But when it is under assault and enemy bombs are already taking their toll, what enervated, perverse antiquities do they not lay bare in the foundations! What things were interred and sacrificed amid magic incantations, what horrible cabinet of curiosities lies there below, where the deepest shafts are reserved for what is most commonplace? In a night of despair I dreamed I was with my first friend from my schooldays, whom I had not seen for decades and had scarcely ever remembered in that time, tempestuously renewing our friendship and brotherhood. But when I awoke it became clear that what despair had brought to light like a detonation was the corpse of that boy, who had been immured as a warning: that whoever one day lives here may in no respect resemble him.'

I think of Ramu when I read these lines. It's of him I think when I reread them. I have no idea why. For one thing, Ramu isn't 'my first friend from my schooldays'

– though he's the only surviving school friend I'll see when I visit Bombay. Bombay: the city I grew up in. The city I grew up in but knew very little. That is, a pretty limited number of roads; specific clusters of buildings.

I feel a deep sadness reading these lines – I can't say why.

When I arrive into Bombay, I make phone calls. This is in the taxi, or the car that's come to receive me from the airport and reach me to wherever it is I'm staying: club or hotel. All the while, I'm registering the unfamiliar: the new flyovers; the disappearance of certain things which weren't quite landmarks but which helped you orient yourself – furniture showrooms; fisherfolk's settlements. I would be surprised – maybe even disappointed – if these large-scale changes did *not* occur. On the right-hand side at the end of the road from the airport towards Mahim is, I know, the mosque with loudspeakers, hemmed in by traffic; on the left, further up, past the brief stink of the sea, will be the church where I once went to attend an NA meeting. I was keeping Ramu company. These aren't parts in which I grew up – but my childhood is coming back to me: the terror – the bewilderment and impatience. The contempt for others. For the city. The magical sense of superiority – like an armour – nurtured inadvertently by your parents: hard to regain.

*

This is a new route. It's very grandiose.

A bridge suspended over water. I've been on it twice before. It is still. In the monsoons, its cables look immovable against the sheets of rain. Suddenly there's an island, low and humped, with irregular houses and a temple, which you never saw on the old route (that route's roughly parallel to this one, which is seaborne). Fisherfolk. No slum. The original islanders – you can't but romanticize them when granted such a glimpse. They were invisible – for perhaps more than a century – from the Mahim side. Maybe they preferred it that way. Maybe they never realized they were invisible. Maybe they don't know they're visible. Of course, they'd have noticed the bridge come up over the years. Children would have grown up and left in the time. Do they leave? It doesn't look like a place to go away from. The houses have a light wash – pale yellow, or pink, or white.

The bridge doesn't last long – it's meant to cut the duration of the journey. When you're on it, you want it – the straight lines, the geometry, the inviolable sterility – to last longer. There are no pedestrians. Everything you claim to miss – human noise, congestion – you cease to miss when you're on the bridge. Death in life.

The other end dumps the cars into Worli. The wrong side of Worli. The car needs to make a U-turn round the potholes. In place of the old sea-facing bungalows, the high buildings for the new rich flank the left. The sea on the right is desolate, though it isn't by the Marine Drive or before the Gateway or even in Juhu. Your first taste of the sea: contained, menacing. Contrary to your desires, you've been deposited in the middle of nowhere – which is what Worli was, and is. Still, the signal has come back – you can make calls again.

Instead, I send out a smarmy text to two acquaintances. 'I'll be doing a reading on the 5th at 6.30 p.m. at . . . And performing on the 6th at 8 p.m. Do come if you're free.' This silly message, bound for people I hardly know, flies out of my mobile as the car turns right towards Haji Ali. I detest messaging. Experiencing any kind of need leads to unease. But I mustn't take the audience for granted.

'Aaj kal mausam kaisa hai?' I ask the driver – the weather's the best subject when you've just released a text and are about to get bored.

At my request, he's turned down the volume of his CD player, which has been broadcasting lushly arranged covers of film songs by a mediocre singer – why covers rather than the originals I don't know, because the latter are easier to procure. Could, maybe, the singer be *him*?

People believe in multitasking in Bombay. It's a word used frequently here.

'Garmi shuru ho gayi hai,' he says, sombre, matter-of-fact. It's March; no vestiges of coolness. Anyway, Bombay has no winter. Everyone knows that, but I get a sense that he thinks I might not know. He's a true-blue 'Mumbaikar'; I'm a tourist – he tests my knowledge by gently asking me my route preferences. He has no idea I grew up here – I, a man collected from the airport – that this city was long ago my life. I'm tempted to share this information, but have no opportunity. Instead, every time the car stops at a light, I stare at the vendors of pirated books who magically appear, who assess you with a piercing gaze as they brandish Jhumpa Lahiri; and the dark girls selling unblemished mogra flowers. White bracelets. 'Bisnes pe aya?' he asks me. I suppose writing is a business. Yes, I'm here on business. But I don't tell him what kind, because I presume he won't understand. What am I up to? If I made millions and entertained millions, there would be a justification; but . . . Nevertheless, I am here, and people, oddly, accept me for what I do. Even the driver would probably be OK with it. Now, the word 'business' – it has such a malleability in the language. 'The business of writing a poem.'

I feel a sense of purposelessness – is it the ennui of the

book tour or book-related visit? Not entirely. No, it per-
tains to Bombay, to being returned to a city where one
performed a function, reluctantly. Reluctance is funda-
mental. You don't plunge into growing up; it happens in
spite of you. Then, one day, it's done: you're 'grown up'.
You go away. Back now in the city of my growing up,
there's nothing more that can happen to me. I embrace
a false busyness. I suppose I'm living life. Without necessarily meaning to. It doesn't occur to me that the visit
is part of my life. I believe I'll *resume* life after it's done.

Ramu. Now, I don't spectate on him as I do on the city:
as a relic of my boyhood. My oldest surviving friend in
Bombay. That makes it sound like the other friends are
dead. But you know what I mean. We argue a lot: it's not
unequivocal affection. He's irritating. I have delusions
of grandeur. But we're both reliable.

Ramu isn't in Bombay. He's in rehab in Alibag. It
sounds like a punitive regime: you can't talk to him
on the phone. He cannot leave. His sister gives me his
news: not that there's any news. She says he went in
voluntarily. The regime will cure him once and for all
of – what was it? It used to be 'brown sugar'; is that still
the fix? The stuff has become 'shit', Ramu once told me,
horribly impure. He's been in Alibag for a year; he'll
be in there for another. Unbelievable! But prevarication

was possible no more. He'd come close to death (I was here at the time) on his first and only overdose (he's a chronic but doubtful user; he flirts with but doesn't revel in danger; he's timid). He lived, courtesy of the kindness of an extraordinary policeman. And a doctor called Shailendra. He lived; he was convinced he'd had some sense knocked into him. He had a certain look on his face for a year. Like a hare that's felt the velocity of a bullet passing a centimetre from its ear. Then, slowly, he became himself. 'How do I look? How do I look?' he asked, narrowing his eyes – he's always keen to know how others see him. And he's also completely indifferent to opinion – a curious paradox. 'You're looking yourself again,' I lied. He had aged, lost some hair, and put on weight. Epitome of middle-class anonymity; he even wore terecot trousers, not jeans. But the self-absorbed expression was back. I was relieved as well as concerned. After a year, he 'slipped' again. He disappeared to rehab without telling me; I didn't know when. I call him very occasionally, when seized by duty or a faint nostalgia. We have nothing really to say to each other, except the usual – his health, drugs, life, Bombay, what he might achieve if he were gainfully employed, masturbation, the girls we knew in school. He makes some cursory but sincere enquiries after my family. He's fond of my parents.

*

The truth is: I've always expected to see him again, whether or not I *wanted* to. I haven't assigned it priority. It's a given. I'll phone him and go to his place when I'm bored in the afternoons. He'll turn up at the hotel I'm staying at, or at the Bombay Gymkhana; I'll sign for him in the visitors' book. Or he'll come to the venue I'm reading at half an hour before the event begins; he'll sit stoically in the audience. Although he's dismissive and impatient, he's quite capable of fortitude. In the evenings, I'll take him out to a dinner or two, sometimes in company, comprising other writers, which makes him restive, and confirms his worst prejudice about 'intellectuals'. I draw the line at times: tell him I can't see him when I have interviews and meetings. I wonder if this makes the relationship exploitative. It's a question submerged at the back of my mind. But it's okay to want friends to be available, right?

Lacan says our subjectivity takes form at the 'mirror stage'. The term and notion are so well worn they might make you laugh – the fate of most revolutionary ideas in psychoanalysis. At around the age of one, we apparently begin to recognize ourselves in the mirror. That tottering toddler is *me*. Lacan points out that our relationship with our image is partly libidinous. Naturally,

I have no memory of first noticing myself in a glass; but I do recall viewing myself pruriently even when I was four or five – making of my twin my sexual play-mate, lingering over him. Handloom House on Dada-bhai Naoroji Road – the place went up in a fire in the eighties. I remember pressing against my reflection as my mother pored over saris.

There must be other leaps in life – as momentous as the 'mirror stage' – that Lacan didn't mention. Some are universal; others, culturally particular. To understand that your parents are human (and not an element of the natural world), that they're separate from you, that they were children once, that they were born and came into the world, is another leap. It's as if you hadn't seen who they were earlier – just as, before you were ten months old, you didn't know it was you in the mirror. This happens when you're sixteen or seventeen. Not long after – maybe a year – you find out your parents will die. It's not as if you haven't encountered death already. But, before now, your precocious mind can't accommodate your parents' death except as an academic nicety – to be dismissed gently as too literary and sentimental. After that day, your parents' dying suddenly becomes simple. It grows clear that you're alone and always have been, though certain convergences start to look miraculous – for instance, between your father, mother, and yourself. Though your parents don't die immediately – what you've had is a realization, not a premonition – you'll carry around this knowledge for their remaining decades or years. You won't think, looking at them, 'You're going to die.' It'll be an unspoken fact of existence. Nothing about them will surprise you any more. My awareness of this fact is never far away on this trip.

Ramu's absence – it's thrown me off-balance and taken me aback a bit. I wonder how to categorize it. Which stage could it be part of?

•◆•

Diagonally across the Kamala Nehru Park is the club. The taxi turns left; this is my destination. The main entrance – I lift my bag up three steps. Actually, the main entrance isn't the right one for guests about to occupy a room. You have to walk down the long verandah (again, on your left) to the reception at the other end to collect your key. Something's going to happen in the evening: PARSI NITE WITH BUFFET AND PERCY KHAMBATTA ON THE ACCORDION.

There's a long sofa here, before which the broadsheets are placed on a table. To these are added, later, the tabloid-size afternoon papers.

Each time I arrive here, I remember. This is where we came – my parents and I – when we left Bombay. I was in Oxford then. But I'd returned on one of my many homecomings and joined forces with my parents in the move. When I say 'leaving', I don't mean we were going on holiday: though I behaved as if we were. We were making our exit. I didn't care: it happened as simply as sloughing off a skin. My parents would be gone, elsewhere – to Calcutta. We had finished our life here, snipped off formal ties. I claimed never to love Bombay. I was making, with my parents, a long-awaited egress. Tired, we came to this club, to spend the last two nights here. My father's flat had been sold; we had no home now in Bombay. The club became a second home – my father was a life member. We were tired but – probably – satisfied, that the money and the property had changed hands. My mother sat down on the sofa before which the broadsheets are kept. Was the reception then on this side, near the main entrance? I recall being visited by a sense of déjà vu on entering the club. I was often getting déjà vu then; I'd felt it when I saw all our possessions – books, furniture, china – being put inside crates. Then, in the club's lobby, I had the faintest of memories: I had *dreamt* of the crates earlier, I'd also dreamt of arriving one afternoon in the club with my parents. This gave me a slight chill: so what I'd had was a premonition of our departure, and the déjà vu was not déjà vu at all, it was the feeling of experiencing what had been foretold in the dreams I had those days, when my parents lived in Bandra and were thinking of departing, and I would return to them in their unresolved state every three or four months. I half smile as this comes back to me.

I nod at the man and the woman who pilot the reception desk. 'How are you?' 'Fine, sir! Your father is OK?' 'He's all right, thank you!' They sway their heads from side to side, denoting satisfaction and closure – more a doll-like vibration than a head movement. They'll ask after my father because he's the member, not I. Where *is* he? The man behind the desk is warmly deferential, the woman is businesslike – the club's female staff aren't unduly forthcoming. I walk past PERCY KHAMBATTA ON THE ACCORDION (wondering if I should slip into Parsi Nite in the evening: I have a weakness for Parsi food) and turn left into the corridor where members are sitting in a cluster of limbs: arms, legs, tennis racquets. Parsis and Gujaratis: a breezy, gregarious bunch. But also oddly clannish. The staff emanate from Deccan soil. When Datta Samant was the guru of the trade unions in the seventies, this club, like every other, was rife with labour–employer warfare. Only part of the tension has to do with class: there's also race and community. The affluent émigrés; the deprived natives. Right now, no one seems to be in a mood to move: the waiters stand in gossipy circles; the members lean towards tables or raise eyes and throw questions at each other.

I remember when this club was nothing: an underpopulated building, a governmental canteen. On Sundays, you'd see three or four members being served rice from a big china bowl, alongside Goa fish curry and ka-chumber. The kitchen was, and is, out of sight; the food and the waiter carrying it on a tray had covered great distances. It's 1970 I'm thinking of. That's when we moved to the tall building, Toledo, that had come up behind the club. Each resident of Toledo – as my father was from 1970 – was given life membership of the club: probably to both increase and improve its clientele. Just as well, because it meant we could use the club as a pied-à-terre or whatever the right term is when we left Bombay, and have been able to continue to use it in that way since. It has changed greatly. Its location in the richest area in the city and the fact that it has no special colonial pedigree means it's both attractive to potential members and less difficult to become one (provided you have the money) than in the older clubs (which, it's rumoured, take no new members). You must keep this in mind as you walk past the people sunk languorously in the cavities of chairs and sofas. They may not be the crème de la crème, but they are rich. Anyway, who's to decide who constitutes the old rich, or if that category is even pertinent here? On certain visits, when I step into the main entrance in the evenings and overhear the din, I'm reminded of Noam Chomsky's incredulous assertion: 'No one parties as much as the Indian upper classes do.' The club has changed again, but that's to do with readjusting the veneer every year: adding granite, changing the name of a restaurant. The core clientele remains the same; so do the basics of the menu: sev puri, chutney sandwich, dhansak, Parsi chutney. When you ask for coffee, there are two options: 'Nescafé', a mound of instant coffee powder in a jar alongside the hot water, or 'filter coffee', a species of South Indian granule that you spot on the bottom of the cup, beneath the swill, or taste as a sediment. If you order tea, the waiter will ask if you like it 'mixed', with water, leaves, milk, and sugar amalgamated into a potion, or 'separate'. I usually opt for 'separate'.

·◆·

I lie back. They've 'refurbished' the room. I loathe the word, its blunt sound (as if someone with a cold were trying to say 'furnished'), and don't use it without irony. But the room is new. Oddly, it's erased the old room from my memory – all I recall is the bathroom, and the plastic bucket that was left under the shower for good measure. I close my eyes. The air conditioning is fixed at 23 degrees centigrade – although there's a remote control on the bedside table, it's symbolic; you can make no alteration to the temperature. Why didn't I accept my hosts' invitation to stay in a new boutique hotel in Apollo Bunder? Perhaps it was the temptation to be an interloper – to spend a few nights, not by proxy but by stealth, in Little Gibbs Road: our address when I was a boy. Close, but not too close. Just to be able to catch a heartbeat. And make my getaway. The refurbished room, with its new bed, prints, mirror, and unfluctuating weather, is more expensive than the old version – but absurdly affordable. I'll claim the expenses, of course. We writers might not earn much by way of fees, but every part of our trip is covered. On tour, we are on loan. We're the pound of flesh that must be repaid in full.

·◆·

With nothing to do, with Ramu absent, I go out for a walk.

Arjun is missing too; he's flown to Delhi to give a talk on the gene. I met him when we were at Oxford. He now runs a government-funded lab on the outskirts of Bombay. He's one of those who, like me, made the decision to return to India. Like me, he couldn't stand the idea of living in the West a single day longer. Unlike me, Arjun hasn't stepped out of India since 1998 – although he's planning to accept an invitation to a conference in Birmingham. I wonder at his lack of eagerness. When we meet up, we rarely discuss serious things; we mostly talk like we were teenagers, or unmarried – as we used to in Oxford. Ramu is suspicious of our candour. He has deemed Arjun an 'intellectual'; the one concession he'll make is, 'He's nice, but horny.' The 'but' is interesting. It contains Ramu's sense of moral superiority. He has many occasions to declare he's morally superior – as an addict, cheated by the city he grew up in; as a non-intellectual; for being less horny than Arjun. But, whenever he carps gently about Arjun, I participate in Ramu's generalizations and implicitly agree. Yes, we *are* less horny than him.

I emerge from the gates of the club on to the main road and glance to my left at Kamala Nehru Park. I feel no time-lag. I catch sight of the park as I used to each day as a boy. Another part of me, hovering a few feet overhead, is studying my situation. Because this is not my life. It could have been, but I chose for it not to be. Instead of turning left, I turn right, deciding to buy toothpaste. Unzipping my toilet bag in the room, I noticed I'd left it behind. So I enter the provisions store. I used to get index finger-sized Cadbury's milk chocolate bars here; they cost a rupee when I was eight years old. I used to love the fact that the bar was so thin and lapidary and would be gone in ten seconds. I barely felt responsible for being the cause of its disappearance. I loved the lettering and sinking my teeth into it. Now, I go up the two steps and find the shop is as busy as if it were Christmas. The Gujaratis within are amenable – they furnish me with Colgate in fifteen seconds. I pay, and consider buying something else – one of the staff is perched on a ladder to retrieve a lotion from the topmost shelf. Everywhere, there is the strain and stretch of trade.

It's a wonder the shop exists. Could it be here because

there's such affluence in Malabar Hill – or is it here despite the wealth? The same could be said of the shops next to it: St Stephen's Store on its right, a confectioner's, and the two grocers' on its left. I first saw them more than four decades ago. Why do the rich give them patronage? Could it be that they want tiny pockets of continuity? Actually, Malabar Hill is an oasis of continuity – its tranquillity is calculated to preserve. When I lived here, I never went into these shops except the one from which I've acquired toothpaste – to get my Cadbury, or watch my mother buy a tin of Kraft cheese. It's only now, as a visitor, that I've discovered St Stephen's Store, and its tissue-thin chutney sandwiches. There are certain things that (obeying orders) I buy for my family when I'm in Bombay, and one or two that I give myself, such as these sandwiches. They're part of my afterlife here.

•◆•

I cross the road. I'm here for the book reading; I've nothing to do this afternoon – or later this evening. I didn't have the wit to notify my friends in advance. But, then, I don't have friends here. The idea is a fiction that I hardly ever bother to examine – which is why I'm often taken by surprise when I find myself at a loose end in Bombay. My mind tells me, 'Bombay is teeming with people you know, or have known.' This doesn't stand up to scrutiny. The people I was close to in school I've lost track of. Except Ramu.

I have crossed the road. Opposite me is the building that came up out of nowhere in the late seventies and partially blocked our view. Before then, we had an unbroken vision of the Arabian Sea. The building is irrelevant to me now, but still causes a pinprick of irritation. It was an interloper – a tenant on the landscape – and continues to be one.

In front of the building, upon the road – there's no pavement here – sits a woman on her haunches, displaying a basket of fruit. What she offers that the grocers' opposite don't, I can't say. In another area, there'd be a gaggle of squatting women. Here, she is one. One is enough for Little Gibbs Road.

Next to her there's a narrow pathway or steps that fall precipitately seaward. Itinerants descend. I catch a blue glimpse of the horizon. I have never been down there. That's because we've spent so much of our lives, even in places we've grown up in, being driven around. Walking, we take expected routes. Even our unexpected routes are well worn. There's much I don't know in Malabar Hill. Like that glimpse of blue.

I feel no nostalgia. What I encounter is an impossibility – of recovering whatever it was that formed me, which I churlishly disowned. Bombay was never good enough for me. Even now – as before – I hesitate to write about it. It is my secret. It was so, even when I lived here. For instance, the Mercedes. My father's white Mercedes-Benz, 'Merk' to my friends. 'Mercheditch' to the proud driver. I rode it but disembarked ten minutes before reaching Elphinstone College. The final bit I covered on foot. Sloughing off my life. And no sooner has the thought suggested itself than I confront the bus terminus near the Kamala Nehru Park. From here ply the 102 and the 106. Red double-decker and single-decker respectively. Sturdy carriers – not like their dere-lict Calcutta counterparts. With the Mercedes presenting itself and escape from it becoming a necessity, I began for the first time to take buses. Incredible cocoon they took me out of. The 106 put me in the middle of the sea-breeze and dropped me close to Elphinstone College. Sometimes, I lugged my guitar along. Fittingly, my hair would be insanely tousled by the time I arrived.

.•.

The Immortals is my fifth novel. It's also my longest one. On paper, it took me nine years to write, although that's misleading. I wasn't writing my new novel all the time. It would have been interesting to have had some sort of a timekeeper to measure the moments I spent writing it. Maybe the total of a year devoted to committing the actual story to the page? Even that seems an excessive span, a phantasmagoric labour. One year! No, I was plotting other things at the time – plotting not the novel, but that resistant tale we call 'life'. At the very end of the millennium, I tried to escape globalization by escaping Britain. I didn't want to go back to a time *before* globalization; I just wanted to get out, move. I moved to Calcutta. Then I tried to escape globalization by taking leave of the novel. I wrote stories. I wrote essays. I composed music. This is what I did a lot of those nine years.

I am in the Kamala Nehru Park. I've entered through the open gates. I love the Kamala Nehru Park, but I didn't frequent it as a child. It served as a landmark: 'We live near Kamala Nehru Park.' Even today, I will – if I'm staying at the club – instruct the taxi driver: 'It's opposite Kamala Nehru Park.' Because everyone seems to know it. I love it, but my discovery of it goes back to a reassessment made in my late teens. Certain things I'd ignored till then, and which had always been close at hand, I began to explore. Among these were Indian classical music, black and white Hindi films, Hindi film songs – and even a place like Kamala Nehru Park. I can't pinpoint what connects these things I've mentioned except that they'd always been in front of me – but I'd never noticed them. They weren't on the curriculum of my upper middle-class life. By the time I was sixteen or seventeen, the outline of that life was loosening, it was being tugged at its edges. I was making those discoveries largely alone.

Kamala Nehru Park's clientele – in fact, Indian tourism – is predominantly working class. We think the working class spends all its time working; actually, recreation is an avid pursuit for wage-earners and 'blue collar' workers. They come to Kamala Nehru Park from faraway localities (Ghatkopar, Mulund) – possibly taking the 106 on the last leg of the expedition. They arrive as families; male friends roam the park in pairs – holding hands: this much hasn't changed. You can spot the upper middle-class person native to this area because the men are in shorts and the women wear trainers. You see them running; one marches past briskly. They return in your direction in seven minutes. The upper middle-class person is an individual; they don't circulate in the park in groups. The visitors from Mulund hardly run; their progress is deliberate. The man of the family is regal in his patience. A family might loll on the grass with a familiarity that resembles ownership. The children run. They rush to the circular raised platform, whose roof beats and vibrates during the monsoons. When a child stamps his foot, there's an answering echo, like a swift, painless slap, special to the podium. All this is as I recall from a year ago, and from forty years ago too. This isn't to say that Bombay is unchanged – Bombay, least changeless of cities! But a few things – like the loud echo here – *are* the same as ever; annunciatory; to be encountered nowhere else.

I like it when I get invitations to read in Bombay – or to give a talk here. Especially as I get so few. No one wants me to read in Bombay. That's an exaggeration. I'm not being singled out. It's just that literary events here are few and far between. It's more likely that I'll get an invitation tomorrow from Abu Dhabi, or Barcelona, or Rangoon. The city belongs to Bollywood. That's what constitutes its imaginative energy, its drive. It has no academia to speak of; its university is now peripheral. And that's why I await the invitation or opportunity – for months, sometimes for a year – with a strange anticipation. It's not that I want to disseminate my work in Bombay. It's just that I long, these days, to visit the city I grew up in.

And who'll come to the reading? I can predict the mix. There might be one or two people whose names I guess at vaguely, but there will be few faces from the past. Few friends from school; few colleagues of my father's. And yet there's a recognizability about the audience – I know them, their clothes and accent. What brings them to my reading? I'm not confident they know me. I'm used to being no one in Bombay – I've experienced years and years of anonymity here, or, more accurately, being an extension of my father's identity. Mr Chaudhuri's son. As was the case at the club earlier. 'How's your dad?' It's a question I'm used to in Bombay.

The park diagonally opposite the Kamala Nehru is called the Hanging Gardens, but it feels to me that Kamala Nehru Park is the one that hangs over the city. Hanging Gardens is situated on a slight elevation on

Malabar Hill; at least, so it seems when you approach it from the club and the Post Office, and climb twenty-odd steps to its gates to find that Hanging Gardens is the top of a plateau. It's more middle class than Kamala Nehru, many more purposeful walkers, their calves bare, socks gathered round ankles. Optimistic foliage sculptures abound: a rhinoceros; a boy on an elephant; a giraffe. These are best ignored. The oddity at the core of Kamala Nehru Park is the great shoe. The rhyme it solemnly provoked when you first saw it as a child was 'There was an old woman who lived in a shoe', mapping the park in your head according to a list of imaginary habitations, of which that abode made of confectionery (which Hansel and Gretel began to eat bits of the moment they found it) was also one. I've never entered the shoe. It's a storey tall; people are always climbing up. I go down paths flanked with flowers – there are so many whose names I don't know; I'm no nature-lover, the only blossoms I'm familiar with are gulmohar and bougainvillea – till I come to the balcony where the park is a promontory overlooking, all at once, the Marine Drive, the eye-hurting glint of the Arabian Sea, bits of Marine Lines, the narrowing at Nariman Point, the clusters of very tall, at times very thin, buildings, the extant gothic towers and turrets and antiquarian domes, and, across all of this, the sea, which extends beyond the Gateway of India. You'd expect a throng here, at this balcony, but it's a manageable crowd. Families; boys straining; fathers complacent; the mothers harangued. Only the little girls look thrilled. Naturally, no denizen of Bombay would come here; at least, none who felt they belonged to the city or had a sense of proprietorship. Which is why I crane to look but try not to take too much time, so others behind me can occupy my place. It's a magnificent scene, an old, old one, which I'd glimpsed from one spot or another in Malabar Hill since I was a child, blankly, appearing to register little; and now, seeing it again, I don't know what to do with it. And so, almost immediately, I turn my back on Bombay, and am now looking at the children who are buzzing before me, who know there's definitely something at hand.

With Bombay and the oncoming evening behind me – the giant pink wash over the sea is expanding – I walk up the red path to the gates and am back at the bus stop again. There's a short-lived agitation in my pocket; the phone's convulsing. I fish it out. The message says: *Don't forget the shoes.* Of course. Something to do! I might have forgotten. I stare and then write: *Remind me of details. Can't recall.* As I proceed to the club, the phone shivers again. *Just take them. Call when you're there.*

They're furled in the suitcase in the room, my wife's shoes and my mother's. Their bones bulge slightly in the cloth bag. I transfer the cloth bag to a plastic one and exit the room. This is my big mission in Bombay, to exchange these bespoke pairs for my mother and wife; either the fit or the colour wasn't right. My mother, even today, approaching her mid-eighties, will wear no other footwear but Joy Shoes. The shop came up in the Taj in the seventies. She became a customer. She's been unflinching in her loyalty. Even now, when she can no longer travel to Bombay, she'll order a pair on the phone. 'Munna?' she says. 'How are you?' in that rich Bengali-accented diction. Munna's a suave operator. 'Hello, madam, hello, madam, all well here. When are you coming next this side?' 'I am not coming but my son is going,' says my mother firmly. 'Please exchange the priya you sent me last time, they are not fitting properly.' 'Send it over, send it over,' he responds breezily. 'Anything else?' 'My daughter-in-law . . .' she repeats these important words, *my daughter-in-law* never wore the kolhapuri she bought last time. Please exchange them for priya.' 'No problem,' says Munna, clearly preoccupied with other things. 'You are size five, right.' 'Four and a half,' she corrects him. 'My daughter-in-law is six,' she adds, though no request was made for this information. Their feet are small, but my mother's are especially tiny, and probably have Joy Shoes sending specifications to workmen for a new pair of priya. At the end of this conversation, my mother and I (who have known him since I was fourteen) are gratified that Munna is alive, given the strange events of 26/11. A close shave. It's been two years. Still, my mother makes sure: 'You are OK?' 'Oh yes, yes!' says Munna, not guessing the association – he's adept at being reassuring.

The taxi driver will test your knowledge. He's planted his car in front of El Cid. The moment I cross the road and say 'Taj Mahal', he perks up: 'Babulnath se jau ya Walkeshwar se jau?' He knows the query about the route is rhetorical. Walkeshwar, I say, meeting his eyes in the mirror. We're soon past the Jain temple, whose striking blue pillars I've only seen from the outside; we've turned round the Teen Batti hairpin, left behind the Governor's house, and are suddenly by the sea. I am now *in* the scene I was looking at earlier; it's the one I stared upon morning and evening from the twelfth-floor balcony. The way to school. By the time I was fourteen, I'd have known this journey couldn't be repeated forever. When I was smaller, there was no end in sight to the morning excursion to class. I took to prayer in the car. The praying was furtive. No one knew about it: not my parents; not the driver. Once a girl in a school bus saw me, and I agonized over whether I'd been discovered. I depended on the Catholic figurines that seemed to hide behind every other corner on the route. My prayers asked for exemption from PE. 'Please let Mr Mazumdar not tell me to run today,' I begged – I wasn't certain if the addressee was 'God'. There was always a saint in waiting. In a traffic jam in Marine Lines, I saw a kindly shape that said 'Our Lady of Dolours' beneath it. I sent the prayer in her direction. This was when, from a neighbouring vantage-point above the car window, the girl saw me. I saw her just after I opened my eyes. Why I was in Marine Lines I don't know. Usually the car went up the flyover and then descended into Dhobi Talao, or went to Churchgate and turned left at the IRAN AIR sign.

As we go down Marine Drive, I see a sign proclaiming NIKHIL CHAGANLAL. I'd missed it before now. Unless it's new. It doesn't *look* new. Could this be the Nikhil Chaganlal who teased me mercilessly in the sixth standard? The sign says he's a painter. That night, I Google him on my laptop. It *is* him. The face matches. He was a scrawny boy; he's better-built now. His 'recent works' includes a series on rooms – mainly bedrooms and sitting rooms. There are no human beings in them, but there's evidence of activity. There's a chessboard on the bed; sitar and tablas by the sofa; a can of Coke on the rug, bright red. The colours have an intolerable gaiety.

The view from the rooms contains the sea – not quite the Bombay sea (it's too blue). The paintings simmer uniformly, as if on a steady, low flame. I am engrossed. I must have presumed (without realizing it) that I'm the only one in that sixth-standard class who's 'famous'. Or at least had artistic ambition.

• ◆ •

There's a great bustle outside the Taj. Once it had to do with the chauffeurs arrayed there, waiting for the sahebs. Now it's the new security regime. The men who brought death here a little more than two years ago disembarked from a dinghy near Cuffe Parade, and then some of them arrived at Apollo Bunder and entered the lobby with guns. To delay the likes of them in the future, you have to put your packages through the X-ray machine and your cellphone in a small coffin-like tray. These Joy shoes of my mother's and my wife's belong, in a sense, as much to the Taj as they do to them. I surrender them to the X-ray tunnel. *Go back to where you came from. Let them accuse you of being dangerous.*

Once inside, I ignore the sofas that, in the centre, form a commoner's court, a diwan-i-am, in which the visitor can be enthroned. This was long the axis of the Taj's new wing. There's something subtly different about the arrangement of the sofas – it's sparser – in comparison to the lot these have replaced and which were presumably destroyed. To the veteran visitor, this loss of continuity is near-unnoticeable; for the new guest, the Taj they see – the busy lobby – is a phoenix risen from the flames. I head for Nalanda. I may as well check if they have a copy of *The Immortals*. The reason for checking is to punish myself. It's not the bookshop it was; besides, its representation of my work is patchy. My visits to Nalanda are coterminous with my trips to Bombay: annual; once in two years. I will ask them straight out, 'Where are my books?', or, if they have one or two allocated to random bookshelves, 'And my other books?' I feel compelled to excavate my titles because I bought books here as a teenager – not just bought books, but lighted on poets I'd never heard of: Tranströmer, then Mandelstam, and Pessoa. The irony of a five-star hotel hosting these elusive men concerned neither the bookshop nor me. Once, I became aware that Sharmila Tagore (smaller than I expected) was standing beside me, the *Faber Book of Contemporary Stories* in her hand, reading, or – from the resistance she emanated delicately – pretending to read. There's little poetry in Nalanda these days: maybe a Palgrave anthology; Tagore; Kapil Sibal. If you're in luck, you might spot Imtiaz Dharker's *Postcards from God*. To my question, the attendant has an all-purpose comeback: 'We just sold out. We have placed order with distributor, but they are not supplying.' If I were to pin down the publishing rep (he's so intangible he's almost non-existent), he will shake his head and confide (I don't know if he's shaking his head, since we're on the phone, but it feels like he is): 'Nalanda balance of payment is very bad, sir. Long backlog of credit. We have stopped supplying till they clear the deficit.' Sceptical, I say, 'That's terrible, Janardhan. The Taj is an important outlet, right?' 'I agree, sir,' he replies blandly. 'I'm trying to rectify it.' 'Do they even know that I've written about the Taj and Nalanda in *The Immortals*?' I say, as if this revelation would alter everything – for me, for the Taj, for Nalanda's plans and my publishers. 'You have written about the Taj, sir?' 'Yes.' There's a small interval. 'I don't think they know, sir. They should definitely know.'

Nalanda is out of copies of *The Immortals*. Says the attendant. He placed an order last month; there's been no movement. Either he's lying – or it's that balance of payment situation; or the distributor's acting up: a long path at the end of which my books lie in a warehouse. But is the distributor a person from Porlock– an invention? If there was no person from Porlock, there would be a person from somewhere else, to make trouble, to come between the writer and their writing. Stevie Smith was right: we *need* our person from Porlock. A voice says: 'It's no one else. It's *you*. Figure it out.' In the meanwhile, as usual, I'm rebuffed. This is not a two-way street, I find. The Taj can be found in *The Immortals*, but *The Immortals* is not to be found in the Taj. I pick up a copy of *Time Out*. This is because I like guidebooks to cities I know.

Out of the bookshop, I'm in the lobby; walking towards the concierge, I turn right into the long corridor. For obvious reasons, they've closed off the side street and backstreet entrances. A part of me regrets this. I wonder if – when the fear and the burden of responsibility this thing has generated have blown over – the doors will be opened again. Every restaurant in the corridor I pass, I make personal and historic notations for: 'This is the Harbour Bar; I was never fully aware of it till Shanbhag of Strand Book Stall took my wife and me there in 1993, and we ate lobster chilli pepper'; 'Here's Golden Dragon (looks different now), where I first encountered chop sticks but never learnt to use them. A few people were killed here.' And, also from the early eighties, this is where I first met Shobha De. It was soon after she'd become a De but before she appended the extra 'a' to her first name. She'd recently married someone who admired my father and lived in the same building as we did then – they took us out to dinner; or did my father take *them* out? The last time

I came to Golden Dragon was in the nineties, during one of my post-marriage trips from Oxford, when my parents lived in Calcutta but we'd coincided in Bombay, and my father brought us here to rehearse past occasions, though I don't think he could afford the prices any more. The manager must have had a memory of him as the incredibly gentlemanly CEO of a big company (though long vanished from these parts) and, at the end of the dinner, charged him nothing. Remembering this, I hold in balance the same emotions I did from fifteen years ago: pleasure, that a man as striking and humane as my father should have been paid tribute to; pleasure, that even in a city as forgetful as this one, people can store away a memory of dignity; pleasure, that he should be acknowledged even when he'd gone from here and, on retirement, forfeited everything, as he'd forfeited his past upon Partition; guilt, that we'd always lived off the fat of the land. To those who have, more shall be given. If you have nothing, even the little you have is taken from you. This is unarguable. But the guilt is a spectre; it has no basis in reality. I wish it to be gone.

As usual, I stop at the photo display. I don't think I'm a celebrity-watcher, but I've always found it arresting. They've returned, affirming continuity: of what was, and will be. The attacks, for them, are just a blink of the eye. In fact, they've been through much more than the attacks. Bill Clinton, John Lennon, V S Naipaul, Nehru. Even Shobhaa De, larger than the rest, Cleopatra-like on a sankheda chair. *They* are the true survivors. They've known the fickleness of fortune, the travesty of renown – and are still with us. For some reason, I think I'll see Hitchcock among them. But Hitchcock never came to India, did he? Still, I forget a little later that he's *not* in the gallery. Which is the one bit of black and white in the corridor.

I press on. Two women of indeterminate nationality – they could be Latin American – walk towards me. They're followed by a middle-aged European in a sleeveless top and skirt. I'm in the foyer of the old wing now, and the swimming pool is on my right. Dusk's falling on the water. I think of Ramu. How, long ago, my parents and I had come here for dinner, and, stepping out later, I'd gone quickly down the pavement (which is cordoned off now by barriers: no pedestrians) and, beneath one of the arches, on the steps of what used to be the chemist's, found Ramu there. It was a year since I'd seen him. I hardly went to college any more, and (this was something I didn't know) neither did he. The year's gap was unremarkable. We were at that stage in our lives when friends were falling off. School friends are like relatives; you can't deny they were part of your growing up, but they come to mean nothing to you. That year, when I saw Ramu on the steps, a couple of our classmates had already gone to America. In the years to follow, others would leave – for Wharton, Carnegie Mellon, MIT. A bit like a wartime exodus. I said to Ramu, 'Hey, what's up? What're you doing here?' 'Nothing yaar,' fugitive in a way that was attractive. I presumed he was smoking marijuana. 'Don't ask.' 'My parents are a few steps behind me,' I said. 'Oh *shit*,' he said, and turned his face towards the arch. 'Rah-moo?' called my mother – she was glimmering in her sari and jewellery. 'How are you?' He stood up reluctantly. 'I'm OK, aunty.' 'Keeping yourself busy?' said my father.

Another time – I think it was 1986, when I rediscovered him in the months I spent in India between graduating from UCL and going back to Oxford – he said he could see himself working as one of the security personnel at the Taj. At this point, he'd been an addict for six or seven years, but was committed neither to being a full-blown goner nor to taking up normal life. 'Normal life' interested him in spurts, but then the enthusiasm for it seemed to vaguely die. The reasons for wanting a job as one of the Taj's security staff were, I think, manifold. First, he believed he looked the part. Also, the fact that, in security, you're doing something while you're not doing very much would have been integral to the job's appeal. Standing smartly, studying the middle distance. And he knew someone who had the job, and this planted the idea in his head. But he didn't know whom to approach or how to apply. The idea remained a possibility.

Before me is Gazdar. Full of the most delicately wrought jewellery. A curlicue of gold on a bangle; the miniature hive of an earring. I have neither the taste nor an eye for jewellery. But, a year ago, I came here to exchange my mother's mangalsutra (just as, now, I'm carrying her shoes). Its beads were like kalonji, or maybe fish roe. Why she wanted to give it up for something else after thirty years I had no idea: an old-age fit or whim. But she's in perfect possession of her senses and her whims have nothing to do with her years. The man at the counter – he was the one person in the shop – claimed he remembered her. I seemed to remember him, because he looked so familiar and appeared to belong firmly somewhere. I asked him if he was Mr Gazdar, and he clarified he was a long-term employee – though he had the ease of a family member, of someone who'd been among the artefacts from a young age, and could regard them as both rarities and objects for trade. He had a slightly uxorious air – of a man who defers to other people's wives because he knows they call the shots. It's not as if Gazdar has hordes of customers, though. I can't afford its wares, but on the day of the mangalsutra exchange I saw a basrai pearl necklace (a fragile exoskeleton that made me nostalgic) which I thought I'd get my wife as an anniversary present.

How come Gazdar escaped ransacking in those three or four days? It doesn't make sense, somehow. I haven't had this conversation with the man who says he isn't Mr Gazdar. What he did tell me, though, is that he shut up shop early that evening – or he'd have been in trouble.

Odd, I think. My mind's gone back to my mother's words. Her recounting to me of her Sylhet days were so vivid that it didn't occur to me that she was unhappy as a child. Even the privations she experienced while growing up had an aura of singularity in her accounts. Sometimes the tearful stories were amusing. Only once or twice did I get a sense of how hard it was. Evenly she'd said: 'I always knew that *that* wasn't going to be my life.' (By *that* she meant both Sylhet and the circumstances her family fell into after her father's death.) And indeed it wasn't. Much of her adult life was here in Bombay, part of it here, in the Taj. 'Your life will be one that you can't imagine now,' an astrologer had predicted. And it was clear, when she told me of the astrologer's words, that she *hadn't* imagined it. She was leading, by then, the life he'd foretold long ago. For me, foreknowledge was similar, but pointed in the opposite direction. This is why I feel a detachment and fraudulence as I walk to Joy Shoes. I knew *this* wouldn't be my life – Malabar Hill, Cuffe Parade, the Taj. 'The streets were never really mine.' I was going to be far away.

'The streets were never really mine.' In a way, this was true of my parents too. Of course, they owned their life in Malabar Hill, presided over it – I loved their benevolent reign. I myself never possessed my time here unequivocally. But when life in Bombay began to unravel after my father's retirement it was interesting how they made almost no attempt to not let it go. It was as if they were used to leaving. They'd left a few times before: on Partition; then to London; then from London. When it came to leaving, they knew how. Not that they were planning to depart Bombay. But on some level they were preparing for departure. And, in acknowledgement, they began to let go of things. My mother anyway liked to give things away. It had been a startling habit ever since I can remember, a tic. She'd gifted furniture to her music teacher, jewels and saris to relations. She even gave furniture to Ramu before we went away – to sell, ostensibly; but they were never sold, and came to adorn Ramu's room. Their last years here were marked by the sale of bits of my mother's jewellery. That's because my father's savings began to run out after retirement; his taxed income had been modest. Besides, he was financing my education in London; he'd borrowed money to buy the post-retirement flat. In 1986, between UCL and going to Oxford, I spent time with them in that small flat they'd moved to in Bandra. Then I got jaundice (though I'm careful to drink boiled water). I was transferred to Nanavati Hospital, to a 'deluxe' room in the old wing. It was terrible. At five in the morning, when I was woken up by a nurse who'd come to change the saline drip, I saw a large cockroach crawl across the floor. That afternoon, my parents moved me to a tip-top luxury room in the new wing of the Nanavati. How? My mother had sold a pair of diamond earrings. Both parents looked excited and vindicated. My father, at this point, saw at least some of my mother's jewellery as one might bonds and debentures: as something meant to be encashed in need. I remember accompanying my parents on two trips into the stifling, entangled maze of Zaveri Bazaar when the bank balance had dipped again. I think it hurt my mother to lose some of those rings and pendants, and I've always wanted to give her something back, but never have. I've long wished to buy her those earrings. But the journeys to Zaveri Bazaar weren't desperate; they were full of anticipation. A thrilling climax. My parents, distracted and happy.

I think we felt that buoyancy not despite Bombay, but because of it. It was a product of the city's high spirits. Buy and sell. The two are ever interconnected. I've not experienced that buoyancy elsewhere.

That idiot Ramu. He often stayed with us then, in those three years when we realized our time in Bombay was ending. I say 'idiot' with affection. Partly I say it because he seemed insensitive to the small upheaval that was occurring in our life. He was immersed in his own upheaval. But he's no idiot. I told him as much as we walked back and forth between the Gateway of India and the Radio Club, the sea black beside us. It was 1986; I was back from London and spending a year with my parents in the flat on St Cyril Road. We often discussed, that year, the possibility of selling the flat – our last pied-à-terre here. Every other day I'd take the local train to Churchgate to wander streets in the parts of the city I'd grown up in and gone to school to, but where my parents no longer lived. It was on one of these sojourns that I ran into Ramu. He told me immediately of his addiction to brown sugar. 'I'm fucked,' he said. We renewed a friendship which, in school, had been neither slight nor thick, but convivial and fractious. He used to call me 'the poet' in school, both to heckle me and pay me a backhanded compliment – not because he'd read my poems but as a response to the fact that I didn't 'do' sports, wore glasses, was maladroit, and kept my hair long. When we ran into each other again in 1986, there was no awkwardness between us. He made a presumption on my time which I was persuaded by. It was during a walk near the Taj that I said to him, 'But you're an intelligent man.' He studied me to check if I was mocking him. 'I know,' he said. 'I'm not stupid. But most stupid people are successful.' I nodded (I too was young). By 'intelligent', I meant the opposite of – a word hardly used these days – shallow. There was an intensity about his bewilderment, his rejection; there always had been. Sometimes the rejection was oppor-tunistic. His problem was boredom, and a sharp need to escape the things that bored him.

Our last days in Bombay were my happiest there – not, however, because I *knew* they were my last days. I had no idea. None of us did. But it was as if a premonition hung over us after the move to Bandra; the possibility of a final and unexpected change. That came soon after my parents settled into the small new flat, the first property they owned in the city. Bandra was so different from everything we'd known. The churches; the remnants of a Goan idea of a neighbourhood; the low – sometimes derelict – cottages. It was as if my father had entered a period of banishment.

When I include myself in the business of leaving Bombay, I ignore the fact that I'd already left. I was in England at the time. In 1986, I took a year off in Bandra, but then went back to England. Yet mentally and emotionally, I was with my parents, and in India. Inwardly, I accompanied and mimicked their shifts in location. The move to England meant less to me than the move to St Cyril Road. Occasionally, I'd discover I was back in Oxford. But I barely noticed this. I was in Bandra. We were gearing up to leave.

Ramu, at the time, was drifting (as I was drifting between countries, pondering the future) in and out of addiction. He'd be clean for six months; then relapse. He'd say, on the phone, that he was 'absolutely fine'; two days later, he'd mutter he'd slipped. I began to feel wary when he said he was 'absolutely fine'. Because when he *was* okay, he merely sounded bored, already taking for granted the ennui of normal existence. The earnestness of 'absolutely fine' indicated that a transgression had taken place. Anyway, even to begin a conversation on the phone with 'How are you?' was to realize it was a loaded question; an interrogation, almost. But there was no way round ordinary courtesies.

No sooner had my parents moved to St Cyril Road than we began to weigh the option – playfully at first – of their selling the apartment and moving to Calcutta. This was to ease my father's steadily growing debt. It wasn't difficult for us to have these discussions, because neither did we think they'd lead to an actual decision, and nor did we feel Bombay was really 'home'. I'd grown up here, but never belonged here. The fact that we were Bengalis prevented us from putting down roots in Bombay, and we underestimated our attachment to it. I say this because later we often missed it deeply. Still, I treasured each day in Bandra. That's because I was back home from Oxford, and every day in that small flat was important to me. I knew I'd have to go to Oxford again, and didn't want to. Bandra flowered around me. It felt familiar to me in a way that Malabar Hill and Cuffe Parade never had. I mean the stray dogs, the infinite afternoons, the low houses – our own flat was on the third storey, from which you could scrutinize the gulmohar blossoms that dominated the summer months at eye level. Every day in Bandra was precious – until I'd pack my bags

again. Ramu would come to stay with me sometimes –
for a day, or for two days, or even (wearing me out) for
three. Our upheaval almost went unnoticed by us – so
why shouldn't it have by him?

·◆·

Cloth bag in hand, I ascend the steps to the glass door. The handles to the doors unite in a horseshoe: the Joy Shoes logo. It's based on a breezy sketch executed by M. F. Husain. Those were the days! Inside, there's a picture Husain painted specially for the shop: one of his incandescent horses. Why an animal that flies off the earth when it runs should be an appropriate symbol for footwear is beyond me. Will these shoes make us fleet-footed? Are they to be hammered into our soles? There's another story here. Husain hardly wore footwear those days. He went around the streets of Bombay barefoot. In school, we relished an anecdote about Husain being refused entry into Willingdon Club because he was shoeless. Hoity-toity rules: serves him right. Someone saw him hopping later on the hot macadam. I enter and see the horse on my left. Husain must be in his nineties now. Ninety-three or -four. Of course, he doesn't live here any more. He's unofficially exiled. Still, why not let the horse hang where it always did? A Husain is a Husain.

'Hello, sir?' says— but his name's gone from my head. 'Exchange, no?'

He smiles and adds: 'When you came back?'

'Just earlier today.'

He shakes his head mildly: not so much a yes as acceptance.

'Mummy OK?'

'She's all right, actually.' In Bombay, you subtly shift your speech so you sound like the one speaking to you. You don't want to stand out. You want to sound more or less like you did when you were twelve: nothing's changed.

'She called,' he says, half smiling.

A woman in a pistachio sari, whose white foot cranes over a shoe, lifts her head. She looks candidly at me. It's a look that one well-to-do person passes prematurely to another.

'Really?'

'Just now only. She was asking if you came. She gave instructions for her shoes and your wife's shoes.'

The woman in the sari looks vindicated; perhaps the shoe fits. There are mirrors everywhere; for us to examine our feet.

I step out discreetly to get a better signal. Not far from me is the palatial back entrance, locked with finality.

'Which colour do you want?' I ask my wife.

'Tell them to bring out the priya,' she advises. She vacillates: 'See what the beige looks like. Also the black. No, actually I have a black one. Check the white. Why don't you decide for yourself? Actually, don't.'

She blames my mother for her reliance on Joy Shoes – they were unknown to her before she got married. Now she wears little else. By the time we met in Oxford, Bombay was history for me: very recent history, but decidedly the past. I revealed my life in it to her piecemeal, guiltily, with a sly boastfulness, conveying, without much effort, how literally incredible it was and also how easily I let it go when I had the chance.

I walk back in. The colours of the classic designs are black, white, gold, and beige. But I've also spotted magenta on the heels. My mother is loyal to the priya. She's incapable of wearing heels; she has a broken foot. My wife, too, abhors heels and the glitzier options. (I pick up a glass slipper and wonder if I can tempt her.) The classic designs don't evolve hugely. Instead, they become distilled. Extraneous bits – which you realize are extraneous after they're gone – are constantly sacrificed; the shoes grow sleeker and sparser.

Munna has appeared. Holding forth into the receiver, behind the till. Busy; but reassuring. I recall he's a Muslim. But why can't I escape this thought? Distracted, he waves. The bonds of mutual loyalty are strong. Is he a Vohra? There are many of them in Bombay; they're prosperous.

'Hello, hello, hello,' he says, in a tone of congratulatory disbelief. 'How are *you*?'

'Haven't seen you in a while,' I concede, patting his shoulder. 'I came here about a year ago for a very short trip' – he nods – 'when my new book came out, but I couldn't come to the shop.'

'But your wife came to take some priya, no?' he asks, his memory razor-sharp. Narrowing his eyes, he says, 'She's not here this time?'

I shake my head. 'No, but she made it a point to send me.'

'That's good, that's good,' he says melodiously, smiles, scratches his beard. 'What's the name of the new book? I'm sure I read about it in the evening papers – or maybe in the *Times*.'

'*The Immortals*.'

'That's it!' he exclaims, glancing at a stub half-submerged in the card machine. The roll's stuck. 'What's it about?' This is a version of the 'How are you?' he's put to me already.

I think of a succinct way of holding his attention. 'You know, I've described Joy Shoes in it.'

'No!' agog, but the steely bit of his attention still fixed on the stub.

'There's a young man in the novel,' I continue, 'comes from an affluent family, but pretends to be poor – wears torn kurtas, frayed jeans, but' – I smile into his eyes – 'he's always in Joy Shoes sandals.'

'Ha!' he cries, wondering what these behavioural traits add up to. 'What is it? It's a novel? Where can I find it?'

Good question, I think, and claim insouciantly, 'Just check in the bookshops.'

No one is sure any more what the novel is. The word has unprecedented currency. People are thrown it intermittently, and sometimes they throw it back. For about a decade now, when I've hedged and said, in answer to some query about my profession, 'I write novels,' people have occasionally countered with, 'Fiction or non-fiction?' Someone said to me that the 'novel' is now confused with the 'book' – it's no longer understood as a form, but as writing itself.

He shakes the roll loose. 'Must get a copy!'

My reason for telling Munna about Joy Shoes in *The Immortals* is not only to elicit a response, or to make him feel like an honour's been bestowed on him. For me (given my writing is accused of coming directly from life), the aftermath of the book, in which people believe they've been written about and start to find their own correspondences, is the most interesting chapter.

'But glad to see all's well! Terrible stuff, what happened.' I've been to Bombay once since November 2008, but feel like I haven't. 'I was watching it on TV in England. Turned on the news. I couldn't believe my eyes.'

'My God!' says Munna, losing his smile. 'We had to go to a wedding that night, so we left early. Usually we begin shutting at eight.' He gestures to his right without moving his eyes. 'Some of those fellows came in from there.'

He focuses.

'Mom's sandals are ready, no?'

'I think he's gone in to check.'

We glance at the room, small as a monk's cell, in which shoes are secreted.

Passing along the corridor, I turn right and come to the majestic red-carpeted staircase. I climb up the stairs; each step is capacious, as if people ascending were expected to make giant strides sideways. There's a lift, but no one in their right mind would enter the shell of the lift when the staircase is available.

At the top of the right-hand stairs, on the left, is what for me is the main, the old, entrance to the Sea Lounge; but this, of course, is closed. Reaching the first floor, the entrance is on the right, diagonally. The Sea Lounge has had to be restored from scratch; it was reopened recently. Once I'm in, I find things have a rehearsed air: the notes on the piano of 'Yesterday Once More'; the spacious sofas inhabited by large groups along the sides and in the centre. I want a table by the window, where only couples sit. There they are, presenting their profiles, painterly against the light. They're deep in themselves. There's a free table by the middle window.

A tall waiter in white shirt and trousers and brown apron escorts me to the table and silently takes my order of Darjeeling tea and a plate of cookies. I don't like Darjeeling tea, but I'm buying time. It's not that far from dinner. Besides, I don't want to spend five hundred rupees on bhel puri. I notice the waiters' uniforms haven't changed. But almost all the waiters are new. In the seventies, the Sea Lounge had a regularity in my consciousness, as my parents used to come here late Saturday morning and occupy one of these tables by the window. Their order, like other things about them at the time, was unvarying: chilli cheese toast, tea. The Sea Lounge had a menu of arcane bites: chicken or mushroom vol au vents, the cream stored beneath volcanic flaps; Scandinavian open sandwiches (the idea of an 'open sandwich', where the filling was left exposed, unprotected, was boldly counterintuitive). Then there was bhel and sev puri, served on pristine china. My mother insisted we couldn't eat these off the pavement for fear of jaundice; but in the Sea Lounge, where they were made in conditions of uncompromising hygiene, her love of bhel was very evident. Sitting at the table, I glance out of the window on my right, while the pianist tinkles away and I follow the notes, reconstituting the words: 'those were such happy times, not so long ago . . . every sha la la la la . . . still shines . . .'

I get up. I know the toilets are far away, and a tour awaits through long corridors. I temporarily abandon the table, leaving the Joy Shoes bag on a chair.

Before stepping out, I eavesdrop on the pianist. A deeply serious man. Reticent, he glances at me, then returns to what looks – even sounds – like a bit of typing. The notes are clunky.

I go through the doors, turn left; this stretch is like a balcony in a theatre. Soon I'm at the inner corridor, where I turn left again; on my right is the Crystal Room – I might have been tempted to wander towards it and peep in, except I know that it's still under construction. Much at this end of the first floor was gutted. That great and useless space must have once, before I was born, been used for celebrations and felicitations, but I only remember its Christmas lunches, weddings, and sari exhibitions. I move away from it. It's a long walk down the corridor to the toilets.

When you come to the end, you feel not so much that you're in another part of the hotel as in a different city. I chance upon an ornate and dishevelled scene. Two handsome liveried men – employees of the hotel – stand watching a band of noisy people in bright clothes: bandhani saris; turbans. Maybe they're wedding guests (poor relations), or the family of musicians or artistes who've come to perform at one of the restaurants. In which dialect are they shouting to each other? I go into the toilet, and a wave of perfectly maintained features – stonework framing basins; antique fittings on taps – engulfs me. I empty my bladder thoroughly. When I emerge, most of the party outside have disbanded – it was only for a moment they'd come together here. A liveried man is fading into the distance.

Quiet has re-established itself with their departure. This is where the rooms are. Quiet, quiet. Beyond the access of interlopers. Those men made for this wing, of course, and the cat and mouse game lasted four days. People fleeing, hiding, dying, changing location at strange hours, led by staff.

The CCTV footage captures flashes of it: the men with guns, intent; the guests and staff transiting at odd times of the night. All of them trapped, circling this wing. It's in the bad lighting of the CCTV video that the hotel echoes the mausoleum it's named after – in which tourists arc round the tombs encased in marble, shrouded in the perpetual semi-dark of mourning, where they can't take pictures. As a result, there's no record of our visits to Mumtaz Mahal and Shah Jahan's resting places. The CCTV footage too, when you see it, seems almost an impossibility.

How long will it take for the Crystal Room to be put together? They must be working on it at this very moment, although, as I turn right, I hear no sound; no hammering, no drilling. I'm back in the Sea Lounge. They've done a good job. It's not so much a twin of the room that was destroyed, or a replacement. What they have tried to do is follow the example of the moving image of the disintegrating object or edifice played backward, so that the shards and fragments, as you keep watching, fly up instantaneously and regain their old places until completion is achieved, and, at last, there's no discontinuity between past and present. Accustomed as we are to technology, we know it's an illusion – the shards are all there somewhere; it's just that the film has been reversed. Is this why Benjamin saw in Klee's *Angelus Novus* (which 'shows an angel looking as though he is about to move away from something he is fixedly contemplating') the 'angel of history'? 'His face is turned toward the past,' he says. 'Where we perceive a chain of events, he sees one single catastrophe which keeps piling wreckage upon wreckage and hurls it in front of his feet. The angel would like to stay, awaken the dead, and make whole what has been smashed. But a storm is blowing from Paradise; it has got caught in his wings with such violence that the angel can no longer close them. This storm irresistibly propels him into the future to which his back is turned, while the pile of debris before him grows skyward.' To be in the Taj is to experience its emergence from this storm. Like the angel, it's turned its back to the future it's once more moving towards. When I look around me in the Sea Lounge, I see its composure and reinstatement – the improvements are so unobtrusive you don't notice them – but I'm also confronting the debris.

'Should I pour the tea, sir?'

But he *will* pour it. There's a rigour to his posture; he stays very straight while the tea trickles out. Three lightly tanned cookies on the plate. I bite one. It turns to powder.

This would have been a good moment to call Ramu. I look out of the window. He lives not far away. It's not like Ramu to consent to a regime that's made him incommunicado; but maybe there was no other remedy.

Ordinarily, I might not feel the need to chat; but the fact that I have no choice except not to is making me restless. Anyway, our conversations are silly; they're designed to return us to our schoolboy personae. It's as if we haven't moved on from those days when we're with each other. I always hated school. Ramu both loved and hated it. All his best years were there, he claims. Yet he hated its glamourizing of sport – not because (like me) he was bad at sport, but because he was so good at it. His housemasters wanted to exploit his abilities – he resisted, to their dismay. They never forgave him. Besides, the school was meant for rich children. Why did his father (he'd asked me), an ordinary middle-class man with a small business, put him in a school meant for the Tatas, the Dubashes, the Ginwallas, the sons and daughters of CEOs, government ministers, and film actresses? Ramu's good at apportioning blame.

I gesture to a man who's standing in my line of vision, by the old exit.

'Bill, please.'

'Yes, sir.'

Before he recedes, I say: 'The Sea Lounge looks good.'

He nods, indulgent.

'But the staff seems new,' I confide.

'Yes, sir,' he agrees, prolonging his puzzled nod.

'Mostly new only.'

'Where's the old staff?'

'Some left.' He hesitates. 'Some died.'

'Died?'

'Yes, sir.' He studies me; pauses, apologetic.

'I see . . .' I fall silent. 'So that's why— But *you've* worked here for a long time. I've seen you before.'

'Thirty years.' He explains: 'I was not here that day.'

When I'm leaving, he's standing by the macaroons.

'Sir,' he says.

I stop.

'I too feel I've seen you before.'

I nod but say nothing. The pianist's at it.

He continues shyly: 'Are you in the High Court?'

I shake my head. Then add: 'My father used to come here a lot many years ago.'

He appears pained, groping – till something alters. His eyes widening, he asks: 'Mr Chaudhuri?'

I'm disbelieving, as if I've glimpsed a ghost. These are the last vestiges of our life here.

'Yes. He's my father.'

'Very good people,' he says, unexpected with this belated certificate. 'Sir and madam.'

*

I go to the other side of the road and face Elephanta.

From the sea came the world. At least, that's how the song put it: 'Prima in Indis, Gateway of India / Door of the East with its face to the West' – words we sang at assembly but never understood. With the armed men having alighted at two different spots from dinghies, the sea hems in the city. It's ineluctable. The city isn't sure what to do with it.

On my right, far away, the Radio Club glows with a wedding. I walk towards it slowly.

The area comes with a history for me. On the one hand, it figured in my father's life. Then, by the time I was fifteen, it begins to unravel. After school, my friend Zainul and I go into the Taj, enter the Shamiana, order cold coffee. When the bill's presented to us, we find we have no money. As I sit, observed warily by waiters, Zainul runs to Arun, whose father lives in a Port Trust flat on this very road, to borrow the necessary sum. He returns after an eternity. When I'm nineteen – not long before going to England – I frequent the sea-front looking for love or a fuck, and never get either. When I'm reacquainted with Ramu in 1985, I become aware of Apollo Bunder's proximity to his house. I see it's dotted with his doubtful landmarks. A small part of it nourishes him – like the overrated kebabs at Bade Mian's. Otherwise, it poisons him: the pushers are here. The arcade adjoining the erstwhile Nanking restaurant is where junkies sit and droop. Opposite Elphinstone College, and especially in front of the Prince of Wales (or Chhatrapati Shivaji) Museum, is where smack – evidently of very poor quality – is supplied at all hours. Parallel to Apollo Bunder, on Colaba Causeway, not far from Electric House is a small church in which there are daily Narcotics Anonymous meetings which Ramu used to deride as being fit for the slow-witted only. Everything Ramu needs and doesn't need is here. He's often complained to me about how he wants to leave Colaba, but can't. Where could he go?

So, in a way, it must be good that he's been extricated, and exiled to – is imprisoned in – Alibag. Maybe I'll hear his side of the story when I see him. I could have walked to his place right now. Enlisted him for tomorrow's reading. I always enlist him. The last time I spoke to him was at the end of 2008, when the city was running amok with terrorists and commandos. ('Terrorist' is one of those terms that, through sheer repetition, has lost all meaning. That is, it could refer to anyone.) Everything was happening incredibly close to his building. 'It's crazy yaar!' he said. 'City's very quiet, and neighbours are telling me smoke's coming out from the Taj. P-police are turning people back when they're coming up Marine Drive!'

I haven't spoken to him since. When I called him in

March, his sister picked up the phone: 'It's a rehab place in Alibag, Amit. He can only speak once a month to immediate family. Yes, he's well. He says he'll be out in a year or two. Yes, a year or two. Thank you for calling, Amit. Your parents are OK? Family? Drop in when you're in Bombay, OK? God bless. Pray for him, he'll be fine.' Ramu's mother was Roman Catholic. The lay expressions of faith underlie his family's blandishments, as they do the Narcotics Anonymous sessions. I recall this; I went to a couple (in the same way Ramu comes to my readings).

Well before I'd written or published a book, and got Ramu to tag along to my events, I was following him – in the late eighties, whenever I was in Bombay – to his NA meetings. There's something to be said for encroaching on bits of a friend's life. You meet new people. There are misunderstandings – someone could accuse you of being there on false pretences. On the first floor of a school in Mahim, an educated-looking man (clearly a recovering addict) making social chit-chat asked me: 'How long have you been clean?' I was cocky. 'I was never on it,' I said. His face darkened, and he moved swiftly on. When I told Ramu later, we both laughed. Such memories! The NA meeting – like the book reading – may not be to everyone's taste. I don't mind it, but Ramu couldn't abide many of the features – the 'sharing', the self-conscious applause, the fist-pumping resolutions, delivered like threats: 'Every day I get better and better.' About the readings he accompanies me to he's more tolerant. To me, the NA meetings were claustrophobic but informal. Ramu finds the questions and answers at book events fairly absorbing. He doesn't mind the droning, self-important recitation of certain passages.

Benjamin's words – 'the first friend from my school-days' – are inaccurate here. My first friend was Jehangir, the gentle Parsi boy who consoled me in the first standard when he saw me crying. I was missing home, which was a short walk away. And there was Shailesh. No one was sure if he'd had polio, but his legs were bent and he wore steel braces and huge shoes; he was smaller than me, but had an ominously large forehead. He claimed the shoes could crush my tormentors. I lost contact with him after he withdrew from school, presumably for his condition. He lived in a building on Malabar Hill not far from where I was growing up – not far from the club I'm staying in on this trip.

I've lost touch with my first friends. But Ramu's the school friend who goes back the longest, to the sixth standard, after he flunked twice and joined us juniors. He became my neighbour in class. The other school friend I see, Anil, has run a series of companies in Britain and lives in Hampstead. I never called Ramu by his first name till we were full-fledged adults; in school, he was 'Reddy'. The word possessed, by association, a certain intractability. His sporting skills encompassed gymnastics and boxing. I remember him springing from parallel bars in front of assembly one morning. Even then he was literally, unhappily, going through the motions. He was short but good-looking; no one could have predicted he'd be six feet tall when he turned seventeen. He soon became better known in school as a flunker and refusenik. He wouldn't be co-opted into sporting activities for the glory of his House. He was quickly demystified for me when we sat next to each other. I regularly beat him at arm wrestling. Others failed in school because they were mentally negligent or disturbed. For Ramu, failure in those days was a bit like a sport. It was the one thing he grew better at. He detested school; being seen to fail gave him authority. He was intransigent, though the teachers heckled him.

'But when I awoke it became clear that what despair had brought to light like a detonation was the corpse of that boy, who had been immured as a warning: that whoever one day lives here may in no respect resemble him.'

'Lives *here*' – is 'here' the city? Or is it the nation? Who's the person who 'may in no respect resemble him', the friend? Is it someone with a new, or different, relationship with the past?

I killed Ramu once. It was in school, after the finals. I killed him in a story. After keeping my literary endeavours to myself, and having them go unnoticed, I had success after the boards. A poem came out in the school magazine, and two stories. The poem was a pastiche of Tagore, called 'Gramercy'. One story was a mystery written in a Wodehousian mode. The other was a tragedy, with an O. Henry-style comeuppance. My doomed protagonist was a boy with a 'coconut-shaped head', and my mother recognized who it was at once. 'Is it Ramu?' I can't recall what the ironic twist was, but the boy was accidentally electrocuted. An end engineered by fate. It was the pinnacle of my literary career.

•◆•

People getting out of cars at the Radio Club are in each other's way: thin young men in sherwanis, women in Banarasis. I turn back. I walk past the Taj and the Yacht Club and knock on the window of one of the taxis by the petrol pump. The CD player's on and the man is staring at the taxi before him.

I don't return to Malabar Hill; I go to the Bombay Gymkhana. The long promenade is empty. Any members here are in the bar. I wave to the one waiter. I order a chicken and vegetable clear soup. My stomach rumbles, but not with hunger; it must be the sandwich I had on the plane. I only eat soup.

By the time I get back, Parsi Nite is ebbing. No accordion to be heard. But people are hovering round the buffet in the dining room. Two men emerge; it takes me a second to realize who they are. Milind Somani, stocky, Savage House, essentially unchanged. The other's more difficult to place, taller, larger, but I know him – Ali Naqvi – from his smile and light eyes.

'Amit?'

I nod and smile at Milind. The night's not quite ended. A woman in a shoulderless dress comes out of the door.

'My God, it's been years, right?'

It occurs to me that Ramu would remember them, because he remembers everyone in school.

'Amit's a writer,' says Milind to Ali, who unostentatiously claims he's aware of this.

They're prosperous, dependable. I envy them. I'm a bit surprised they know what I do. Not because I don't think Milind reads, but because your closest circles generally hear what you do last of all: your family, your childhood friends, your city, your country. In reverse order.

At night, in the sealed dark of my room, I dream of going to the Hanging Gardens.

•◆•

The morning is washed by light. Most of the waiters on the ground-floor verandah are already bored. But two or three look keyed up with fresh purpose. I order toast and tea. 'Pudina chai,' I say.

He reappears in a little while with a lavish number of slices wrapped in tissue. The toast is already buttered, and in the clutter of spoons and plates is a tiny container of jam.

I lift the lid off the pot and peer in. There's a shrub with mint leaves swimming inside.

'I have an interview at eleven,' I say, cradling the mobile phone to my ear. I mention the name of the paper. 'I'm bored,' I say. I stir the tea with my other hand.

'Why?' asks my wife, incredulous. She thinks that being in Bombay is enough to make me bubble with excitement, that I don't have a moment to think. But I find this time that – not having planned in advance, and discounting the interview, the bookshop visit arranged by the publishing rep, and the reading – if Ramu and Arjun are both absent, I have little to do with my day.

'Where's Arjun?'

'He's in Delhi to speak about genes,' I say morosely.

I decide to walk up the stairs to my room and glimpse, through the latticed wall, the building in which I grew up. It isn't as if I'd forgotten it; it's just that I see no point in looking at it directly. I know it exists at the back of the club, but it's a surprise to chance this morning on its continuance. The time's ten fifteen. The journalist will be here soon. It's that dead time, when you're waiting for something that's neither entirely productive nor significant, but is supposed to be necessary. While you wait, you can neither write, nor think of writing, nor of the last book or the one you're embarked on, nor go shopping. I defer returning to the room.

I step out into the driveway. Lazily, I let my eyes go over that familiar width and height. It needs a coat of paint. It's never departed its first colour scheme: white and mustard. I was eight when we moved there. I looked down from the balcony every day, in times of boredom or unhappiness or those long stretches when I was liberated from unhappiness. To look down is unlike looking up. You encompass what you see. You can make a journey – as I did, with my eyes, to Nariman Point, where my father's office was. To look is to dream. Or it's to relive with dread a physical journey, as I did on Sundays, tracing with my eyes the curve of the Marine Drive to Churchgate – my daily school route. The eye covers distances in a second. It lusts for freedom. Looking out, I often wanted to be free – not of home, but of the city. The eye (if it's gazing upon something it's unhappy with, as I was) might see nothing.

Looking up is different. I have the freedom I then wanted. I'm free of Bombay. I have no home here. Looking up is hard work; before long, you encounter an intolerable brightness, or emptiness. I squint and count the floors. 'One, two, three, four . . .' I was on the twelfth. 'Six, seven . . .' I think I counted the same floor twice. I start again. Then my gaze alights on a balcony. I'm not sure it's the right one. Anyway, there's no mark to identify it with. I strain to see. My home.

This area subdued the terror of the world by ensconcing me, and imparting a terror of its own. The terror of education. The kindergarten I went to is down the road, a two-minute walk. It's been converted into an enigmatic fortification that has no immediate use. I lived then not in the building opposite, but in another one five minutes away, in a corner adjoining the far end of Hanging Gardens. Tenerife. In kindergarten, I stood all morning by the entrance and waited for my mother to walk back.

From Tenerife I was able to spectate on the bee-buzz

of a playground of another school, the school I'd eventually go to. It's almost diagonally opposite the kindergarten. It's the infant section, and the smartness of its design means it must have arisen in the fifties. The Junior, Middle, and Senior schools near Flora Fountain are, in comparison, dour – they're neo-gothic – and may go back to the nineteenth century. The playground is, of course, smaller than I imagined it as a child. Ramu and I went not long ago and peered through the gate in the evening, marvelling at the power it had over us.

I haven't forgotten something that Ramu said as we paused, wonderstruck, at the main gate. There was not a sound within. Much of Malabar Hill, despite the incursion of vendors around the two parks, is an idyll. Little Gibbs Road especially so. At its core, the Infant School and the fairy-tale principal's house next door – we nudged each other when we saw it – is an oasis, a continuum. Ramu was staring into the heart of the idyll.

'It's not for everyone,' he concluded.

'What?' I asked.

We'd been slagging off teachers, sounding off without affection about people we'd known in school who'd gone on to become global managers or CEOs, or had married each other, or had simply given up and died (there were a few of those too); we were complaining about the false values emanating from our education. Then, staring, we fell silent – unusual with Ramu, because he's incapable of keeping quiet. We were both, now, immune to school. Or were we? Did the playground and the long corridor running at a right angle to the empty front porch still exercise, as we stood looking, a kind of mastery? I was unsettled by memory but felt essentially grounded, and unmoved: I lived in another city; I'd married someone who wasn't from these parts. My childhood had metamorphosed into something other than mere, logical adulthood and taken me out of Malabar Hill and Bombay. What of Ramu? I couldn't second-guess his thinking.

'What's not for everyone?'

'Life,' he said, and this broke the spell. We turned, and walked into the lane going right, towards the steps to Hanging Gardens and Kamala Nehru Park. 'It's not *everyone's* cup of tea.'

He was forty-eight years old, a recovering addict, and I suppose he had the right to strike a note of dissent. It isn't one you hear frequently. Since there's no choice in the matter, you automatically assume life must be an excellent thing: it's your fault if it isn't. Ramu's words reminded me this is a dogma. We can't declare at some point that we aren't fully invested in life, because there's no option but to be invested in it. During our time in the world – fifty or sixty or eighty years – we simply pretend we've decided to be exactly where we are.

．◆．

I'm embraced by a smell. There's an enormous kitchen in the basement. Curry leaves. I turn my back to the building and go back in.

I revisit my room, which is dark till I insert the key ring into its niche. The air conditioner starts to hum and the lights come on. Someone has made the bed and wiped the floor and pushed my sandals to the side of the dressing table. The Joy Shoes bag is where I put it last night – by the suitcase. I could part the curtains, let the light in, but there's no view – just the edge of the pool.

I lie back in an amphibious posture, feet on the floor. Unable to read, I imagine the neighbourhood disperse around me. I'm waiting for the journalist. However, if I'm downstairs, seated in expectancy, it'll be bad form; so I must either time my descent so that I come out when he's in the lobby, or listen to the air conditioning till a text arrives. Where's *The Immortals*? I think it's in the suitcase. I don't normally carry a copy because it takes up space. I borrow it from the display stack for sale, return it when the reading's done. But distribution has been so erratic that I've had to be self-reliant. Should I glance at the pages? I baulk at what I might find. Besides, must I ready myself for interviews and readings by consulting the novel? Surely the onus should be on the journalist? There was a time, not long ago at all, when they'd arrive out of breath, and slip in, in the first minute or two, 'Sorry, the book reached me very late, I couldn't read it,' or just 'Sorry, I haven't been able to read the novel,' and you were meant to understand that, on the list of things to be surmounted in this person's day, your book was near the bottom. You then had to describe the book from scratch – its characters; its impetus (or 'inspiration'); its story. You found yourself under-performing. Not having read it, the person would circle round subjects you had no competence in: India's new-found success; *The God of Small Things*; the recent rise of Indian writing. At day's end, this poor man would mould the tête-à-tête into an account of India's onward march.

I can't put my finger on the reason, but most journalists today finish the book. The desperation has passed. Sometimes a conversation is possible.

It takes everything in me to be still till it's eleven. Then I rise.

In the foyer, I'm startled by the bold fragrance of vada; then the sour stink of sambar swims briefly towards me.

Waiting for my man. My eye lights on a newspaper. I missed one this morning, but the cold turkey didn't last long. Already, in two hours, the news on the front page looks irrelevant, as Orpheus had become to Eurydice when he turned round. I glance at the headlines. Kasab. They've been wondering what to do with him. They're going to kill him, of course. Sentenced a few months ago. When he was discovered in Chowpatty, he pretended to be dead. Then he wanted treatment: 'I don't want to die' – the life-urge waking in him fiercely. Later, his inclination changed: 'I don't want to live.'

The paper's edges rattle. A waiter drifts to the next table: plate heaped with sev puri.

'Sir?'

Ah, this must be my man! He's embarrassed – or is he just uncomfortable meeting me?

'You're Nilanjan?'

'Yes, sir. Sorry, sir. There was a problem with my train.'

'Where do you live?'

'Malad.'

When I was a boy, people knew Malad as they knew Jupiter. Today, every other person is from Malad or Mulund. The city I grew up in, called 'Bombay' then, is now 'South Bombay'. Only those with inherited wealth live here. The staff live in quarters and outhouses. The middle class live in Malad or Mulund. Or further afield (like me), in Calcutta or England. We make short trips to South Bombay.

'You got off at VT?'

'No, Churchgate, sir.'

'You come every day?'

As we talk, I take him to a table near the main entrance, where the smell of vada is near-absent. The ceiling fan battens the air at great speed. He deposits his bag and unzips it.

'Only on Mondays, Wednesdays, and Thursdays. I came today because they said you're leaving tomorrow.' He looks up from the bag, smiles. Retrieves a gadget.

'Yes, I have to get back.' He doesn't know that I'm sometimes in two minds about staying on. When I was a child, I missed Calcutta so much I'd pray for the holidays to come. Then, at the close of summer vacations in Calcutta, I'd literally pray for the flight home to be cancelled. Only once did God listen and such a disruption take place. I haven't forgotten that unexplained bit of largesse; the journey back to Pratapaditya Road and my uncle's house; the homecoming – because I thought of Calcutta as home – all over again; the spectacle I made of myself in my unfettered joy. That's how much I resisted Bombay then.

'How much time does it take you?'

'To Churchgate? An hour.'

'That's not too bad.'

It takes an hour if you're coming in from Bandra, from Juhu, from the airport, from Andheri West – and from Malad. An hour to reach the gothic terminuses; the glowing hotels; Chowpatty Beach; the roundabout at Flora Fountain. An hour's a symbolic duration.

'You've lived in Malad for long?'

I lead life vicariously. The young man fascinates me. I envy this daily closeness to Bombay.

'Two years, sir.'

His surname could make him Punjabi or Rajasthani. Or Bengali.

'I came here from Kolkata.'

Ah. That accounts for the dishevellment. It's more than today's onerous journey. But I also envy him his new life in Malad. The grind. The excitement of commuting to the city. The exhaustion and uncertainty later.

'Should we sit here?'

He presses a switch and a red speck begins to burn. He places the gadget at a polite distance.

'You don't mind if I record this?'

'I'd be happier if you did.'

Smiling, he begins.

'It's nine years since you published your last novel. Why the gap?'

A premeditated query. Yet I'm flattered at his concern.

'I suddenly grew tired of the novel,' I confess. 'No more, I thought. I returned to India from Britain in 1999. And I asked myself, "Must I produce a novel every other year? Can't I take a sabbatical? Does every experience I have need to be addressed by this one form?"'

As a backup, he's taken out a notebook and ballpoint. He starts to scribble.

I feel a surge of bile against a genre that's squatted on the writer's life for two decades – demanded submission; determined failure and success; defined the writer's sense of worth or lack of it. I'm a novelist, but at some point I've been – as they might say these days in US Intelligence – 'turned'. I pretend; bide my time. And, when I can, undermine the genre I work with – or for.

'It's your longest book, no, sir?'

'It's gigantic by my standards.' Leaning against the tinted glass of the restaurant, a waiter who knows me by sight is idly speculating. Club employees have a bit of the custodian in them. They make me nervous for no reason. I'm not sure if press interviews are permitted on the premises or if I have to write a letter to the secretary. 'This is a proper novel, I think.' Nilanjan nods eagerly. 'It took me a while, but I *finally* think I've learnt how to write novels.'

He looks up.

'How do you mean?'

'I'm thinking of Frank O'Connor' – the waiter shifts his gaze – 'who said that the poem or the short story is about the . . . the *moment*, and the novel – I think he had the nineteenth-century novel in mind – about the passage of time. You can follow the arc that characters' lives make in a novel, almost from birth to youth to adulthood to old age to the time of death. Over the novel's duration, you're witness to a flowering and attrition. The poem gives you a beginning endlessly. It represents a fascination with openings. It never wants to move, in effect, beyond the first paragraph: the magic of the start. It's a kind of addiction. The short story writer too must have experienced that addiction somewhat, and never recovered. The novelist says, "The beginning is done; I must get on with it."'

'And *The Immortals*?' he asks.

'It's more a novel, right?' I take stock. 'Though there are, by O'Connor's guidelines, short stories that do the job novels are supposed to: give us a sense of a lifetime having passed. I'm thinking of Maupassant. You remember the story in our school reader? "The Necklace"? I read it in the eighth standard.' He nods. 'A succinct tale. But by the time you've reached the end and realized the mistake the woman's made, you get a sense of an entire life lived and possibly wasted. Length and brevity are matters of perception, and, when you realize at the end of many years that you were tortured by a delusion, those years might seem insubstantial, as they do at the end of "The Necklace". Maupassant is good at doing in two pages what a novelist might achieve over four hundred. I'm thinking of something quite short, maybe a page and a half, called "A Day in the Country", in which two couples are described (petit bourgeois holiday-makers in a French village, not unlike people you see today in Puri or Sarnath), and their tics, compulsions, emotions. Then, at the end, there's a leap of fifteen years into the future, and a two-line coda about what happened to the holiday-makers. You grasp a lifetime in that story. By O'Connor's formulation, it *could* be called a novel.'

He subjects the gadget to a nervous scholarly stare.

'Just checking,' he says, sheepish. 'I once did an interview and found nothing was recorded.'

Ting. Ting. Spoons.

'Want to see if it's all right? Better to do it now.'

'OK.'

He fondles a switch. Presses rewind. At first, it's the club we hear; the lobby reduced to a hiss. Then my voice, unbelievably earnest and self-regarding, like a young priest's. The words near-incomprehensible.

'It's fine.' He smiles.

'Should we continue?'

'How much of the novel is autobiographical, sir?' He pushes the machine a few centimetres towards me.

Well, this had to come up. A stock question, but thrown at me with a certain punctiliousness.

'I don't like the word "autobiography".'

'Why, sir?'

'Because I'm not really interested in telling you about my life. The term indicates that I am.'

Nilanjan looks worried.

'Of course, I've described this neighbourhood in the novel, and' – I gesture, lifting an arm – 'I did grow up here.'

A waiter looks undecided at my movement. He's unsure if I want to place an order.

'But that's beside the point. The reason Nirmalya spends part of his life here is not because I want to give out information about myself.' He's making notes again. 'The genre of "autobiography" presumes you first live your life and then pour it into a piece of writing. But Barthes – Roland Barthes?' – Nilanjan doesn't deny knowing the man – 'says that you'd be wrong to think that Proust based his character Charlus on a man called Montesquiou. Barthes believed that Montesquiou modelled his life on Charlus.'

Nilanjan looks up sharply.

'So this idea that life doesn't have to *precede* writing starts to make sense. Have you noticed that, when you're immersed in a book, it takes a while to come out of it when you look up? If the novel is set in 1915, you'll find the room and street you're in will belong for a couple of minutes to 1915. Writing generates life.'

A bearded man in a kurta stumbles towards our table.

'Ashwin!'

'Sorry I'm late.' He glances at his watch to check if this is true.

'Ashwin is the photographer,' says Nilanjan.

'Hi, Ashwin.'

He ducks his head. 'Sorry, got held up.'

Lowering his voice, as if Ashwin's appearance had introduced an illicit element so far absent from the interview, Nilanjan asks: 'Do you mind if he takes photographs? While we talk?' They exchange a look. Impossible to read.

'No problem.'

Bending behind the wicker chair as if for camouflage, Ashwin focuses his camera.

'Who or what do you think the real protagonist of your novel is?' asks Nilanjan soothingly, as if his main concern now is to distract me from the photographer. 'Is it Nirmalya – is it Shyam Lal – or is it music?'

'I was exploring a misunderstanding in the novel –

between Nirmalya and his music teacher. A misunderstanding with a hint of tragicomedy.' I hear a click: it throws me. But not in a way I'm unused to. I breathe deeply. 'Nirmalya belongs to *this* world.' Again, I wave my hand without precision. I feel thirsty. 'But he hates it. He pretends to be poor. He won't be driven around in a Mercedes. He wears torn kurtas. But he doesn't give up on Joy Shoes sandals.' I smile, but Nilanjan hasn't caught the reference. 'Nirmalya can't figure out why Shyam Lal, a great singer, a man from a traditional music family, wants to make inroads *here*' – I indicate my environment – 'a world Nirmalya – a typical teenager in some ways – thinks is completely superficial.' The term 'South Bombay' has very recently entered my vocabulary, but not with enough authority for me to use it now. 'On the other hand, Shyam Lal is puzzled by Nirmalya. He's proud the rich ladies of Malabar Hill want to learn singing from him. He can't see, really, why Nirmalya is sullen about the life he's so lucky to have.'

The clicking punctuates my words every ten or twelve seconds, frequently accelerating into a frantic whirring.

'The comedy comes from how Nirmalya becomes his teacher's instructor. "You must change your life" is his baneful teenage message to Shyam Lal. One thing I learnt while writing the book is that the novel is a form in which you can mock that message (given that

Nirmalya is the one saying it) without diluting its urgency.'

When our conversation peters out, Ashwin suggests we change location.

'One or two pictures in another side of the club,' he says, pointing to the path skirting the swimming pool. It appears to lead to a little wood. No, a small playground, with swings.

I step out into the sun and smell chlorine and water. Ashwin asks me to lean against a tree. Behind him is the building in which I grew up; too bright to look at the higher floors. He takes a picture, then steps forward to adjust my chin, turning it to the right. I have surrendered to him. Photographers are the new Brahmins: we have no volition when they rule us. 'Perfect,' says Ashwin, releasing a fresh burst of clicking.

We head now in the opposite direction. We're at the main entrance, tennis courts on the far right, an outhouse in front of me. I could see both from my balcony. The brisk tennis players, getting out of their cars with their racquets. Dark ball boys surrogating as their tennis partners. Ashwin asks me to stand by the wall separating the courts from the driveway. He gets down on one knee. He's taken a couple when he finds himself obstructing an incoming Honda. He rises; the security guard waves prohibitively. I make my way back and stand by the outhouse. How I envied its daily goings-on! The girls who lowered keys in buckets. The sloping roofs. Ashwin and Nilanjan are conferring. I still don't know who occupies its rooms: club employees; the people who work in the shops on the main road; the adjoining mansions' staff. Even the cat lying on the ledge has more room than I ever did in Malabar Hill.

•◆•

I adore Parsi food. After Nilanjan and Ashwin leave, I talk to Janardhan, the rep, and we decide to meet at the Britannia Restaurant. When I was growing up here, I waited for invitations to Navjot ceremonies and Parsi weddings. There was no other way of tasting that food. Even now, I'm not sure what 'Navjot' is, but guess it's a coming-of-age moment, equivalent to what the sacred thread ceremony would have been to a Brahmin boy.

I thought there were no Parsi restaurants. I kept waiting for wedding and Navjot invitations. I concluded that Parsis, like Goans and Bengalis, were inept at marketing their cuisine. It's true those restaurants were few and far between. But they did exist. It's just that I didn't know them. I was so ignorant of Bombay. One, for instance – Paradise Café – is close to Ramu's house, on the opposite side of the street. I had no idea. Now I've tasted its food and even witnessed its renovation. Ramu took me there to eat sali boti and caramel custard.

It seems to me that Bombay doesn't know me, as a writer or person; that I must find readers here. But, also, it seems I don't know Bombay; I must have looked the other way when I was in it. What else can explain my previous unawareness of places I eat at these days, now that I don't live here: Paradise; Jimmy Boy's; Britannia? It's not that I didn't try to find them. I remember hearing, on one of my trips back from England, that the Ratan Tata Institute on Hughes Road had opened a Parsi restaurant. Finally! So we set out on that nearly hour-long journey, my parents and I, from Bandra to RTI, charged with anticipation for kid gosht and dhansak. On reaching there we discovered the place was closed. Ah, Parsi food and me! Our paths, those days, seemed destined never to intersect.

•◆•

I'm hungry.

'Britannia,' I say to the taxi driver.

His face in the mirror is expressionless. He doesn't want to come out and say he doesn't know.

'Ballard Estate.' He turns the ignition on.

Britannia is not a Parsi restaurant. I'm told it's Irani. The difference isn't clear. Iranis and Parsis are both Zoroastrian. Except for the 'berry puḷao' on Britannia's menu, the cuisines are identical. The thought of the pulao animates my alimentary juices. I feel a pang.

There was no Britannia Restaurant for my parents and me. I lit upon it in conversations a few years ago, when I was visiting Bombay and going on about Parsi food. 'Open only for lunch,' they cautioned. It took me two years to make time to eat there. Now, when we're in Ballard Estate and ask for directions at the Mint, a part of me feels a bit stupid about how late I've been reaching this place. I began looking for it years ago; it was here all along. The feeling of foolishness won't go away.

*

Janardhan is among the gathering on the pavement. Our names are on the waiting list. He shakes my hand; smiles joyfully. 'We're number three, sir,' he tells me. 'He said ten–fifteen minutes,' indicating the shambolic man conducting table placements and issuing orders from a dark desk. 'Too crowded.' Britannia is in the Lonely Planet guide.

Most of the time Janardhan travels in Maharashtra, selling textbooks and blockbusters to outlets in small towns, possibly putting in a good word for me. He sees I'm different from the blockbuster writers. Mysteriously, I'm fairly well known, though my books don't sell in large numbers. It's got something to do with my reputation 'abroad', this inexplicable position I occupy: he senses this, with a vague curiosity and regard. He also recognizes I'm incidental to the business. He thinks I'm a throwback. It would be a cliché to claim that our relationship would have been the same had he been dealing in pulses and I were a supplier. It matters to him that I'm a writer. That's because there's a writer in him. I feel the writer stir – ingenuous, shrewd – when we spend time together.

I've actually only seen him once before. We liked each other instantly.

'How's your friend, sir?' He puts the question to me when we're seated.

I'm looking at the menu. I already know what to order.

My friend? Of course. Janardhan's one of the many who were introduced to Ramu in the course of my readings here.

'Ramu?' I say.

'Haa, Ramu!' he cries, delighted to hear the name.

Their conversations were competitive at first. That's not just to do with Ramu's possessiveness (he's competitive with my wife, and once told me: 'I've known you for much longer than she has'); it comes from his bias against strangers, from keeping to himself too much. Janardhan noticed Ramu was at a loose end. It amused him. Ramu is incredibly sensitive, and might have imagined Janardhan was amused even if he wasn't. He bristled – he felt he was superior to Janardhan.

'He's out of town.'

Janardhan erases his smile.

'Very nice man.'

Yes, he'd grown fond of him. And was entertained to see Ramu hanging out with me – like *he* was. He with a purpose, Ramu without. There was bound to be empathy between the two. The way they stood together at Crossword's.

'Mineral water?' asks a waiter, pausing adroitly in the middle of zipping around.

'Fresh lime soda,' I tell him. I'm tempted to have a

Pallonji Raspberry for its ruby-red colour.

Janardhan looks conflicted. 'Plain water.'

Our silliness. Ramu's and mine. Janardhan an on-looker. Our lapsing into Baldy's voice. Baldy said things with a quaver; frequently underlined observations with 'C'mon yaar!' Baldy was a fantasist; he wanted things constantly. 'C'mon yaar!' He was from an incredibly rich family, but they couldn't give him what he craved: girlfriends; lavish parties; sporting glory; good grades to mark his true intellectual level. All these he fitfully fantasized about. Those who knew him also knew he was a dedicated masturbator. He discovered porn – the small Danish magazines – quite early. Money helped. The word for masturbation was 'shagging' – a quasi-comical activity, like belching or farting, except it was more taboo and more necessary than these. You had to be despo to shag; yet all the boys did. The girls wer-en't privy to this ecology, this single-minded pursuit. I never saw Baldy after leaving school. He had to exit early, after failing his prelims. We must have chatted on the phone, because he told me he'd joined a tutorial school called Cambridge. (All tutorial colleges for dropouts had names like Cambridge, Oxford, and Har-vard.) He was excited, because it was air conditioned: 'It's AC yaar!' By then I was bored of him. I speak of him in the past tense as he died in his twenties of cocaine abuse. Ramu and I have no memory of when we began to use Baldy's persona to address each other. It's wholly unconscious. Sometimes the spell is broken; we see what we're doing. 'Shit,' says Ramu. 'Poor guy.' Because Baldy was lovely. In his urgent way, he wanted everything. We say a few words as a requiem. At what point we resume speaking with that quaver we don't know. We no longer think of it as Baldy's. It's a primordial voice; goes way back into our past together. Very Bombay; couldn't possibly sound right elsewhere. Janardhan saw a bit of that tomfoolery and smiled.

'Order?' The man in white has made his routine stop.

'Vegetarian berry pulao?' I say to Janardhan.

He's vegetarian. Daal roti is his staple.

'Yes, yes.'

'Anything else?'

He shakes his head and looks terribly shy.

'I'll have a mutton berry pulao. And fried bombil.'

Bombil is a late discovery. When I lived here, I knew the sundried version, flattened strips of Bombay Duck, which you can smell a mile away. We called it shutki and ate it to a searing East Bengali recipe. I saw what bombil really looks like when Adil Jussawalla introduced me to my first Parsi restaurant three years ago. Jimmy Boy. He took me to lunch. I'd read *Missing Person* as a teenager. He ordered fried bombil. I ordered saas nu machhi.

I'd last eaten it two decades ago at a wedding. When the food came, I became transfixed by Adil's bombil. Slim, browned, crisp – I ascertained casually that this was the fish I'd known as Bombay Duck. I couldn't focus on the pomfret in the translucent sauce. But I wasn't brave enough to ask Adil for a morsel.

Later, stomachs full, we walked towards Horniman Circle. I was unhappy. I didn't know when I'd be in Bombay next, or see bombil again. I thought I was familiar with Horniman Circle, but hadn't heard of the name. Who was Horniman? Adil said he was a Jewish benefactor. Skirting the curve of the garden, we began to talk about Parsis. The dwindling numbers; the choice they were presented with, of marrying one another or opening up to other communities and diluting themselves. Either way, they'd go. When I was a child, they were a given. Their pale skins, the surnames denoting professions, their musicality of speech, their skill with Mozart and Brahms. 'Frankly, I don't care,' said Adil. 'Sorry?' 'I don't care if they vanish.' It was as if he were speaking of a brand of chocolate, or a railway route. I noticed his use of the 'they': as if being a poet had freed him. We headed towards Strand Book Stall – where I'm due again today.

Plates plonked before us without warning. Munificent

brown rice; berries shot through it like pomegranate seeds.

Just ahead of me, on the right, is a portrait of Queen Elizabeth. The proprietor (I see him floating around the tables) is a fan. He's been ninety for years. He'll soon be at our table to confirm that we've ordered, and address us as 'Young man!' Wiry; restive. All who eat here will be treated to his love of the royal family. They'll hear him out, be charmed – by him, if not the memory of Empire. Then they'll go back to their plates.

'Interview was OK?' Janardhan scoops up rice. He has the distant air of a matchmaker who's brought together two parties and is interested only if there was any acrimony between them.

'I think so.'

My concern has to do with how it will be transcribed. There was a time when journalists had you say what they wanted you to say. You winced, but no one else noticed. People only remember the picture.

'What's the photographer's name?'

Janardhan hesitates, his spoon half-raised. Light doesn't dawn.

'Ashwin!' I say after two seconds. We return to the berry pulao. I'm not sure if I should stalk him, and ask him to consult me before he sends off a photo for publication. I have – I feel – been historically too hands off about the angles at which I've been shot.

Bombil! On a small plastic plate.

'You don't eat fish?' I treat vegetarianism as a phase that might any second end without warning.

He shakes his head.

The backbone is almost as soft as the flesh. I attempt to separate the two. Ever since I confronted those biscuit-gold specimens in Jimmy Boy, I make certain I don't leave without tasting the white flesh. I've noticed it's covered by a film of slime which in another fish would be repugnant. They're gone very quickly.

•◆•

By the time we reach Strand Book Stall, I never want to think of food again. This is not a book signing; it's an impromptu visit organized by Janardhan. Nevertheless, they've placed a stack of *The Immortals* on a table. I start signing, my back receiving a blast of cold air.

Shanbhag died two years ago. I met him here when *Afternoon Raag* was published. I had no idea he was a legend or even *who* he was. I realized I was being presented. 'He created the bookshop,' a distributor whispered. I turned into the schoolboy who used to come here once. School didn't seem very long ago in 1993. *Afternoon Raag* was my second novel; I didn't feel like a writer, though I wanted to be treated like one. 'You like Chinese food?' said Shanbhag. 'You eat lobster?' He took my wife to the Captain's Bar at the Taj and ordered lobster salt and pepper. The bar was dark.

Signing done, I'm drawn to the titles around me. It's difficult to manoeuvre within; books take up most of the space.

But I'm sensing a petering out. Is it to do with a

change of direction? Next to my novel is piled a book on the Buddha I've never heard of, and next to that a pile of horoscopes.

I have, at home, an anthology that I bought from Strand Book Stall when I was eighteen. Renée and T. Weiss's *Contemporary Poetry*. I remember eyeing it, picking it up, coveting it. I wanted it for the names: C. P. Cavafy, A. R. Ammons, Hans Magnus Enzensberger. I let a year pass before parting with whatever the equivalent of seven dollars fifty was that year. It was a magical time. You read what you pleased.

'Finding any good books, sir?' asks Janardhan at my shoulder.

'Some. When I was fifteen, I came here for James Hadley Chase.' I can't say if Janardhan knows Hadley Chase. We read him to be grown up. It was the sex that marked him as a serious writer, as it had Nick Carter. At fifteen, I had no inkling of Cavafy and poetry. That would come the following year.

'You came often, sir?'

'Almost every day after school. It's ten minutes away. Cathedral.' He nods, sombre.

I turn to the passage at the back, linger before sociology texts and a smattering of recent Indian novels, and come out onto the other side of the small room. The location of the poetry section is still the bottom shelves on the right. There's a steel chair here.

I sit and peer below. Chaucer. W. H. Auden. The three shelves are full, but the range is curtailed. I see some friends and acquaintances. Ranjit Hoskote. Anand Thakore. Arundhathi Subramaniam. The last two were in the group that accompanied me to dinner a year and a half ago. After a reading. Ramu was there; he made no secret of the fact that he felt uncomfortable with the poets. We went into the back streets of Kala Ghoda to dine at Trishna. Naturally, no tables were available. Ramu dissuaded us from waiting outside and plugged Apurva. So we had that celebratory meal at Apurva, and Ramu didn't let me order pomfret because he claimed rawas is a better fish – this is quite expected. I don't eat pomfret when I'm with Ramu because he prefers rawas and surmai. He hardly eats out. I seldom eat pomfret these days because you don't get good pomfret in Calcutta. People think I must love fish because I'm a Bengali, but the truth is that, having grown up in Bombay, I only eat sea fish – I generally abhor the freshwater fish you get in Calcutta. In Bombay, I order pomfret when I can. But Ramu won't let me; he's convinced I'm going to be converted to rawas, which is what we ordered that night at Apurva – flat grilled pieces like bits of wood.

•◆•

I step out, book in one hand. It's *Six Memos for the Next Millennium*. Some books I buy for their title, others for brevity. I love short books – the way you know from the first page that it's going to end.

'So I'll see you at six fifteen?'

The reading is at six thirty. We've been speculating on the possible size of the audience. It's hard to shepherd people into readings in Bombay.

Janardhan shakes his head in agreement. It's half past three.

I cross the road. Stacks of sugarcane being pulped by an old flecked grinder. Three flattened bouquets. Pale green juice. High risk of jaundice if you drink a glass.

That meal at Apurva. I haven't seen Ramu since. I've often thought of my last sighting of him, in front of the Yacht Club at night. It's only occurred to me now that – of course – it was after the reading, that abortive jaunt to Trishna, the rawas at Apurva. A long table; Ramu making semi-serious conversation with Arundhathi; Arundhathi's steely indifference when Anand burst into a raga; Anand and Menaka suddenly talking to each other, mildly combative, in French. Later, the contingent began to walk to Regal Cinema. Not that late: eleven o'clock. Through the dark arcade. Anand following one demonstration of a raga with another. We lost Ramu and a young short story writer called Sumit. For seven or eight minutes, they were absent. Then, as we came to the wide angles of Kala Ghoda, they emerged from a back street, sheepish and triumphant. Fair weather friends. I couldn't tell if they'd had a joint, or if Ramu was still 'clean'.

People began to get into the silently lined and watching taxis. It's odd how unselfconscious and at home people are in this part of the city, but how, come midnight, they'll start returning to Juhu and Bandra, an hour away. Waves and farewells. Yet two or three of us decided to catch a final glimpse of Apollo Bunder. Ramu was terribly tired and opted out. I suspected he'd had enough of the writers. 'Fuck, it was an effort to lift one foot after another,' he told me on the phone the next day. 'It was as if the distance from Rhythm House to Regal was a mile! I was wondering when it would end.' He'd parked his scooter at the Yacht Club; we said bye to him there. A part of me felt bad – don't know why – leaving him. As if I were deserting him. Ramu, prodding the pedal repeatedly with one foot till the familiar racket began. Under a gothic arch. I thought I'd see him again, somehow.

The uncertainty I feel – about whether I'll see Ramu again – came to me once before. Of course, I know the formulation is absurd. It's not *whether* I'll see him, but when. According to his sister, it will be another year. What I feel isn't so much like parental anxiety. With the prolonged absence of a child, say, the irrational part of the parent's brain will rush to the possibility of never seeing the child again. This isn't what I feel. I *know* I'll see Ramu again. But it's *as if* I won't see him again. I'm thrown off-balance – but also surprised. I didn't know I'd react like this. Ramu isn't the only close friend I have. But it's as if my sojourn in Bombay *depends* on him. 'Depends' is the wrong word: I haven't come here *because* of him, to delve into his whereabouts. But the surprise I've mentioned is related to my astonishment at being here. 'Astonishment' denotes how you might start seeing things you hadn't noticed earlier, but it could also mean becoming aware that you won't see them again. As I turn into Pherozeshah Mehta Road and then left into the long stretch of DN Road, I know I won't see Bombay again. That is, I *will* see Bombay again, but not the Bombay I'm looking at now.

I belch and release the ghost of bombil. I need this

walk. The first time I had that hunch – that my sighting of Ramu when I said bye to him had a finality that neither he nor I was fully aware of, though in a way both of us were – was at GT Hospital, the psychiatric wing. He'd almost died, but – as the doctor said – had returned to life, against medical logic. I was in Bombay, again, for a cultural festival. Again, I was in the Yacht Club. (If the hosts won't put me up in a good hotel, I'll ask to stay in a club that's well located.) The event was in Bandra; later, I, Arjun, Ramu, and Amrita (whom Ramu and I knew from college, and were seeing after twenty years) thought we'd go to a seafood restaurant. But Ramu broke away early, reminding us it took an hour to get to Colaba. I was headed there too, but not yet. He set out on his scooter and at some point must have changed his mind and decided to check out the entrance of the Prince of Wales Museum for pushers at midnight. He overdosed there on dodgy heroin, and, when a constable discovered him at 3 a.m., his blood pressure was near zero. This nameless constable found a friend's number on a piece of paper in Ramu's wallet; called him; the friend phoned Ramu's father. Ramu's father had to run down Colaba Causeway because there were no taxis to be seen at 3.30. He got his (unconscious) son to GT Hospital. The rooms at the Yacht Club are cavernous, but the skylights have no curtains; I was woken by an orange glow above me. Thankfully, day begins late in Bombay. By and by, I called Ramu. A maid with no Hindi kept picking up the phone. She instructed me in Marathi that Ramu was in the hospital. I wondered if his father had fallen ill; he was then eighty years old. In the evening, at long last, I spoke to Ramu's father. He related the sequence to me. I said I'd go to GT Hospital the next day. I didn't know where GT Hospital was. I was told it was next to Crawford Market. I'd been to Crawford Market as a child, a willing accomplice in my parents' expeditions to gather alphonso mangoes or track down Bombay Duck, or to go from there in the heat to the alleys of Zaveri Bazaar to browse gold jewellery. In the morning, I found GT Hospital in the midst of this: I hadn't known. I went into a driveway. I confronted an unostentatious colonial structure. Bombay doesn't know me, but, also, there's so much of Bombay I've just begun to know. Through the corridors I went to ICU 2; families on a bench outside; a girl in a salwar kameez reading the Bible, the page open at Samuel. He'd come back from the dead, the young doctor – an intern from a small town – told me; it defied reason. I loved the hospital – its resolute calm, its ability to accommodate, even in the bustling main stairways, droves of family members and well-wishers. When he got better, Ramu showed the doctor an interview with me that had appeared the previous day in the *Times of*

India – with a photo of me, squinting in the sunlight on Carter Road. 'This is very good,' said the doctor, moving his head in consternation, as if he'd examined something infinitely stranger than a medical report, 'very good.' They moved Ramu two days later to the psychiatric ward – compulsory, because of the overdose. All free of charge. I marvelled at these easy, unimpeded transitions from ward to ward. Every room there had the depth and width inherent in rooms in buildings the British left behind. Most people in the ward were labouring people and workers. When I went to see Ramu, they were all quietly eating lunch. Not Ramu; he was awaiting a tiffin carrier from home. We sat on his bed, talked and, strangest of all, treated the surroundings as normal: strange for us, ordinarily so intolerant. Yet I was astonished, coming face to face with the obvious and unimaginable. Everyone was in a gown that came down to the calves. I stayed for twenty minutes; I had a flight that afternoon. When Ramu stood up, the incongruity of the gown became painfully clear. I ignored it and we never mentioned the hospital clothing. We said bye very easily, too easily, as if, for the first time, we'd weighed the notion of not setting eyes on each other again, that this moment in the ridiculous gown would be the last one we'd share – and dismissed the thought at once.

•◆•

DN Road! Some of the buildings are a century old. On the pavement and in the arcade, hawkers. The imitation Longines watches and cheap sunglasses and faux-leather wallets. The purveyors of VHS tapes and audio cassettes have been ousted by cell phone repair shops. On the pavement, far below me, are misshapen figures: a girl on a cycle traversing a wire, one end to another; a green boy doing back flips. Toys. The dark eyes of the kneeling vendor who's just released the spring and given them jerky life make contact with mine.

Suddenly, light and noise flood in. I'm at Hutatma Chowk. Flora Fountain is before me. I wait to cross.

Reaching the side on the left, I enter the ruined arcade leading to Homi and Baliwalla. I see more than I once did. For instance, just before entering the crumbling arcade, I notice floral patterns on the wall below a first-floor balcony. They're above eye level, as if they weren't meant to be seen. Why they were put there is beyond me. Somebody's fancy. Like some of the sculpted figures, occupying far corners, ensconced round each other in Konark. Almost as if you were supposed to overlook them.

Ramu loves these buildings. Our being able to understand and express this love speaks to the distance we've travelled from school, when Flora Fountain simply meant school was near, and spelled daily irrevocable doom. No more. That patina of fear, and then functionality, has lifted. Two years ago, I was here in Bombay, and Ramu and I were walking (after dinner at Mahesh Lunch Home) past Flora Fountain to Churchgate. Humanity was receding, inasmuch as it recedes in this city. We were discussing in tones of outrage the prices at Mahesh, and beginning to agree their steepness was Lonely Planet's doing. Heedless of Flora, we turned to study the buildings behind us – as you'd turn, say, to look at the full moon. They were beautiful. Partly illuminated. I shared some jargon with him. 'That one's art deco. See? And *that* has some neoclassical elements.' Open-mouthed, we drank them. Then, wheeling round, resuming our walk towards Churchgate, we crossed at a light, and Ramu pointed at a gothic phantom on the left, opposite the Central Telegraph Office. 'I get *transformed* when I see these, yaar!' he exclaimed, waving at the shadows. 'They take me back to a different time and way of life! Sometimes I even stop and look at the ironwork on the fucking gate – it's mind-blowing!'

Ramu's vocabulary is unusual. Like the word 'transformed'. I wasn't wholly surprised, but did register it. 'Trans' – across; a movement across form; change. I know that recognizability is an illusion. Nothing is fixed: not Ramu, in terecotton trousers, hair thinning, deceptively turned out as a nine-to-five office-goer; not as he was thirty years ago, thin, in blue jeans, with a beautiful but disbelieving face; or in school, short, introspective, unassimilated. The Ramu I see isn't Ramu. He is 'transformed'.

The building was abandoned, but intact. We considered the black railings, tapering into exquisite, thick points. Victorian. We're both fantasists. We need to be taken out of who and where we are. What we see prompts in us not a desire for the thing itself, but another time and place. 'Shit,' said Ramu. 'Just look at that.'

Bandra. 1986, 1987. Two, three years prior to my parents' departure. In '87 I went to Oxford. That small, pretty, third-floor apartment my parents moved to, facing the lane. Ramu would come and stay with me for three or four days. He'd run out of a change of clothes; begin to don my thin white kurtas. He's only two inches taller than me; they fitted him fine. He said he felt no craving to 'use' when he stayed with us. He was an onlooker and eavesdropper on our discussions about departure, saying little to persuade us one way or another. I used to wonder sometimes when he'd go, this kurta-clad figure. He'd slip the moment he returned to Colaba. Then he'd be unreachable for days, and I'd start to forget him.

In St Cyril Road, he and I quarrelled often. Or, late at night, we'd watch a porn VHS he'd brought with him. Or, with the peculiar stoic solidarity he displays at readings, he'd listen to me do riyaaz.

We'd go for walks. Both of us in those white kurtas. St Cyril Road. St Leo Road. Pali Hill. Being fractious. The main point of contention was whether the girl who'd walked past was looking at him or me. 'She was looking at me,' I'd say. 'D'you think she's blind?' he'd reply. 'Why would she look at you?' My last years in Bombay. This precious wastage of time.

And we'd stop to stare at the houses. Churches. Walls. The 'cottages' and 'villas' built by Christians. They were being torn down one by one to make way for buildings. The value of property per square foot made no sense. 'Look at that,' he'd say, and we'd stop and, not speaking at all, imbibe the verandah, the open window, the roof, the palm trees, the rocking chair. This was when we were in communion; when we stopped talking and acknowledged this desire – not to own (that would be impossible) but to imagine.

*

One night after dinner, we made our habitual trip to Carter Road, to the promontory bordered by waves. Near Gold Mist Apartments. Couples sat here, ruminating, day and night; dogs barked and fucked each other before them.

We progressed towards Perry Road. He pointed up to a white smear on the sky, as if the light of the moon had revealed a smudge on a surface. 'See that?' I narrowed my eyes at the expanse. Suspicious of infinity. 'That's the end of the Milky Way. Veeru told me.' Referring to one, a young filmmaker, who dabbled in the environment and astronomy. 'That's where another universe begins.' I checked to see I wasn't dreaming up the faint smudge. How come the sky was so bright?

There's a line, or veil − beyond it, another world. We sensed it then, on St Cyril Road and Carter Road: a house on the street; a streak of white in the sky. It was like a semi-transparent pane of glass.

On this trip, there's a veil too.

•◆•

Behind the veil is Ramu. I can see him. He reappeared in 2011 – in the summer. I called his house, expecting to speak to his sister; he picked up the phone. 'Fuck! When did you get back?' 'I called you yaar – two months ago. It kept saying "This number is not reachable" or some shit. I was going to call again.' Is he bullshitting? Then I remember I was in England at the time. He tells me how horrible the regime was; how he was beaten and locked up. I feel appalled, briefly reliving his terror. 'How did you get out?' It's been one of my objectives in life never to go near anything reminiscent of school again; it might account for my shyness, for years, about getting a job. Ramu never liked school, but used to be nostalgic for the order it brought to his existence. 'I was allowed to get a call from my sister once a month.' 'Yes, I know.' 'I t-told her I'd had enough. I told her what was happening.' 'Then?' 'She and my father came and got me out. Fuck! I think I should lodge an F-F-FIR, yaar!'

He never completed the two-year rehab. It ended three months ahead of schedule.

'Are you coming to Kala Ghoda?'

The festival. He'll invariably ask the question, come January.

I may be in Dubai, I say. So, possibly not. I hear him out – how more than half his life's gone, how he's un-used to being 'clean'; he's unprepared for life. Experien-tially, he's eighteen. He's almost fifty-five. We change tone, expatiate on how shagging derails our lives. I call him in a few days – Dubai has been cancelled. Plans have changed. So I've said yes to Kala Ghoda.

'They're putting me up at the Astoria,' I tell him. 'What is it?'

It's an implausible name. The festival doesn't have enough money to send you to the five stars, but they assign you to uncommon locations. I could ask for the Yacht Club, but the thought of Churchgate is inviting. All I want to make sure of is that it has no rats.

'I know Astoria,' says Ramu. He knows everything about this environment. 'It's near Eros. It's OK – it's good. Like not fantastic or anything, but good. I can check it out.'

'Good is all I need. You don't need to check it out. Ask Ali.' Ali is in the hotel business – a manager. Went to the same school as we did. I remember his 'house'. But I didn't know him. He's a recovered addict. Close to Ramu.

The next day, Ramu calls. 'He says it's fine. Not like the Taj, but good middle-of-the-road hotel. I can check it out.'

Almost immediately upon arriving at the Astoria in the afternoon, I need to go out and meet an art historian. I call Ramu (he has a mobile now). But I can't see him until later in the evening. This is the way things are when Ramu's around. I don't give him priority. He's what survives of the familiar here – he's what I don't need to think of, unless he's absent.

The historian is part Indian, part Polish. Her name is Radhika; she returns frequently to Bombay. We meet up in a café near the Yacht Club, in the arcade in which junkies once huddled together, now plush with restaurants. I'm struck by how beautiful people in the café are, while noting the price of the baked yoghurt.

The yoghurt comes in different flavours in an array of little clay bowls. I didn't have a proper lunch on the plane. I invite her to share. She digs into the one mottled with blueberry. I tell her I want to see the Bhau Daji Lad Museum. I've heard so much about it.

'Ah, I'm going there tomorrow!' She knows her way around Bombay better than I do. 'Which is why I will miss your talk.' She raises an eyebrow in annoyance. 'I have a meeting. I asked them to change the timing – but no!'

I'm not going to the festival, though I know a couple of friends are reading this afternoon. It's a seven-minute walk from the café. People from all over Bombay are going to swarm the triangle between Max Mueller Bhavan and Rhythm House. Ramu lives fifteen minutes away. He never goes unless I'm reading.

Coming out of the café, Radhika and I stroll together to the Gateway of India, and here we part ways. She turns right into a by-lane to return to her boutique hotel in the pathways behind Apollo Bunder. I continue up the sea-front, towards the Radio Club. Though I'm not at all far from where Ramu lives – I need to turn right, then left, and the building with the Ganesh Photography Studio sign on the ground floor will soon appear – I call him and we arrange to see each other at the Astoria at seven.

Naturally, things have changed in the last four and a half years since he's come back. He has a cell phone. Impossible to think he could be familiar with a gadget, but he's inseparable from it. I hardly call his landline any more, which his father picked up exclusively the day long as the gatekeeper to the family: 'Yes, Ramu has *just* gone out'; 'Ramu is sleeping'. I have a smartphone myself. My wife made me buy it. I blame her. I depend on it, and loathe it intensely.

Our fathers have gone. Mine died over two years ago. This life, which I'm revisiting, was his life. I think of my past here as my parents' creation. It wasn't mine. Ramu's died last month. He fell, broke his hip, had to be operated on, went into a coma shortly after coming to consciousness after the operation, when he shouted at his family and insisted he wanted to go home right away. Being the son, Ramu took the decision about taking him off life-support and the ventilator. 'He was brain dead,' Ramu told me. 'He wasn't alive, yaar!' He sounded lost and defiant.

Tall, loping Kannadiga. Six foot two. Picked up the phone after it rang four or five times and said a prolonged 'Hellooooo?' Slept on a bed nearby.

In my overnight bag in the Astoria are priya chappals. The control model, on which I must base a new purchase. Munna has hinted to my mother on the phone that this particular style of priya is extinct. She's not interested. She can hardly walk without support after the knee operation. Her courtship of the priya has to do with a single-minded pursuit that defines the sort of person she is, rather than a need. Munna won't question it.

*

On my way back, I disregard my instinct, wade into the human cross-current before Jehangir Art Gallery. They've come to stare at installations. I wish to access Rhythm House. It's closing down. It'll be gone next time. I dance out of the way of the festival melee, push the glass door. I recall exactly what it was like inside when I was a boy. When places take on new incarnations, I find it difficult to summon up their earlier ones. But with Rhythm House the memory of the vertical stacks of records and the booths in which my friends and I listened to music without buying, averting the staff's accusatory glances, dominates the hazy thing it's been for twenty years: this hive of CDs. I expect a crowd inside, taking advantage of final clearance, but find it's a semi-lit warren leading nowhere.

I'm undecided about the time we live in. This ongoing passage to oblivion. The disappearance of things you took for granted. Then there's the renaissance of things you never knew of, or presumed you'd never see again. All the songs I could have listened to in Rhythm House, and more, I find on YouTube. And bombil is suddenly a part of my life. And Trishna, which I heard of only ten years ago, I now make a pilgrimage to on every visit.

•◆•

I left the hotel after keeping my bag inside, so I hardly saw the room. It's nice. Wooden floorboards (or is it linoleum?). Thick white curtains to compensate for the fact that it has no view.

I wanted to stay here because it's an art deco building. And because it's Churchgate. I couldn't imagine what it means to spend the night at Churchgate.

I invite Ramu to give it the once-over. He comes up in the lift. Although the room's on the first floor, you don't take the stairs, and you tend to obey the liftman when he tells you to step in.

'This is what I'd expect a room here to be like,' he observes, standing by the bed, looking round him, taking responsibility. His hair is thinner than last time. He looks settled and respectable. 'It's good.'

'It's good,' I echo.

We turn to leave. We proceed through the corridor, realizing it's here – outside the rooms – that the hotel's presence can be sensed. We opt for the stairs. Before even attempting the first step downward, we discuss the stair-case.

'Fuck,' says Ramu. 'Look at that space!'

I know why he's agitated. There's an opening-up here, dim and clean, corresponding to the lightness we feel inside.

'W-where you'll get that in modern buildings?' he challenges me, querulous.

Although it's fairly early for dinner, we notice the restaurants as we walk towards Marine Drive. I was never on this boulevard in my growing-up years at this time of the day – in the light rising after dusk. For some reason I feel I live round the corner. In fact, it's like I've been here all my life. This unspoken sense of belonging to Churchgate doesn't dilute my encounter with it. 'Look at that!' K. Rustom and Sons. People biting into ice cream sandwiched by two brittle wafers. A ghostly congregation. 'I don't believe it,' says Ramu. I thought it had slipped into history. What's difficult to account for is that it's identical to what we remember.

We walk past Pizza by the Bay – once Not Just Jazz by the Bay – which I went to with my parents when it was Talk of the Town. I remember the polite nervous-ness with which we watched askance, eyelids blinking, a couple pirouette and dance the Salsa. Since then, I've only ever seen this place from a car, a few seconds at a time. We cross; we're at the sea. We turn our back to it. We sit. We don't bother with the men in t-shirts on our left and discreetly turn away from the Muslim couple on our right (they must be Muslim – the woman is delicate and beautiful).

We catch our breath and study two edifices – the Talk of the Town building and the Iran Air building. We lean, propped on our palms. I identify the style, mention the curves and vertical lines that mark out art deco – not because it explains anything or helps us better understand our rapture, but because it's always pleasurable to talk about something you like.

'Achha,' says Ramu as I talk. He can be compliant. 'Achha.'

We began to note the Marine Drive houses one day not long ago in a car, going towards Nariman Point, glancing left – I must have come in for the launch of *Calcutta*. He was two years back from his terrible stint in Alibag (which he never believed he'd escape) and this was a new lease of life for him in a city he'd detested, and he was seeing it with new eyes. 'Beautiful,' he said, peering as houses flitted past. We observed this flank curving on the left, ignoring the sea, as if the panorama had no relevance – as if the houses held the key to

how life might be lived here. I felt a repressed nig-
gle as I stared. Suddenly, I said, 'Look at the windows.'
'Huh?' Then he saw it too. 'Fuck, you're right.' Frame
after aluminium frame had replaced the casements. The
gesture by which you push a window open was now
unnecessary. 'Fuck,' he said glumly. It was as if a part
of us that was air and breeze had been denied entry.
Resentful, temporarily silenced, we gazed, for the next
five minutes, upon the swift, unvarying succession of
aluminium frames travelling the opposite way.

•◆•

Soon, restive, because we're not tourists, we get our backsides off the parapet and begin to walk back to Churchgate.

I demand Parsi food. He isn't surprised, but exercised. 'Where we'll get Parsi food here?' he cries, as if we're in the middle of a desert. But he's not one to give up. 'Stadium Restaurant,' he says. 'Cheap grub, but good. They have Parsi food also – sali boti, patra nu machhi.' We laugh; the names are intrinsically funny, the way he says them. But we're happy too soon – the Stadium Restaurant offers Parsi dishes on Tuesdays only. Momentarily lost, we proceed to Flora Fountain. We don't want to end up at Mahesh Lunch Home. Also, I don't want him to wander pointlessly. He had jaundice three months ago. His liver's a bit off. 'I'm absolutely fine yaar,' he says. 'I have a huge appetite these days.' We do end up at Mahesh Lunch Home. Since he won't partake of a large tandoori pomfret, I ask for a small one, which is modest-looking and below par. He has grilled rawas. We agree the daal is astonishing. I take several spoonfuls before he finishes it all by himself – he's unstoppable when the mood takes him.

Bombay! The city never tires, but, returning to Church-gate and the Astoria (where his scooter's parked), he's fatigued, and plops down on one of those beautiful green benches you wouldn't notice but which adorn the footpath leading to Eros. It's only eleven o'clock. I take a picture of him: to send to my wife, to share the moment, and to prove incontrovertibly that I'm up to no mis-chief. I'm not confident of my chances in this light. But the smartphone is adept, and I capture a fair likeness of him in the nocturnal glow between Flora Fountain and Churchgate, staring at me aloofly. I then do what I've done only once before, with my wife on Christmas Day – take a selfie with him; two, to be safe. My lips are parted, as if I'm poking a dead thing to see if it'll come to life; it's the phone I'm attempting to keep at a dis-tance. He's smiling faintly, as if amused by some exotic piece of wildlife. Although this is Bombay, where the weather never changes, there's a coolness that makes me protective of my singing voice: so he's lent me his grey sleeveless sweater, which is like a covering of mud on my shirt. My wife will ask me later what it is I'm wearing.

*

Only drunks stare at statues. But here we are, remarking on the figures as we edge towards Eros. At night, it's less desirable to pretend they're not there. What do the dogs make of them, who know them daily? Ramu's got his breath back; we're a few minutes from the hotel. I never liked the statues keeping vigil, primarily because they were too close to life. Now we're both ready to grant them a moment. 'Who's this bawa?' asks Ramu loudly, sizing up the walrus moustaches of a man in a topi and robes. Any great man memorialized in this way he assumes is a Parsi. 'Fucker must've done a lot for Bombay at one time,' he concludes. 'We need people like this today.' It's not a Parsi; it's a Hindu. Mahadev Govind Ranade. Leaving aside his air of self-importance, he looks marginally foreign, as all the statues do. Which is why Ramu takes them for Parsis. It's a simple confusion. We're not drunk – Ramu has hardly touched alcohol since he left Alibag. We pay sober respects to these personages who no longer belong – maybe they never did. We leave Ranade fronting the Oval Maidan and catch a glimpse of the Astoria.

•◆•

I sleep: deep, interrupted sleep. The Astoria is my home. I've caught myself saying twice to Ramu, 'Well, I should head home.' I've heard others say the same thing in the evening when they've come to a city. Occasionally – not always – they correct themselves. This is what 'home' is: a place to return to at night.

Book tours have their bonuses, which don't necessarily have to do with the event itself. Mine is the fact that I'm about to fall asleep in Churchgate. I can't hear a thing. The lack of sound is extraordinary. Tomorrow I will wake and walk to the Asiatic Stores. I need some antacid.

I'm a family man – I don't want to be single. But, hypothetically, if I'd been single, I'd have liked to live in a hotel room rather than in a flat or house. That *is* a fantasy. The predictability of living in a given space in the centre of a city. The thought will occur to me sometimes. To *live* in the Astoria. I could do it, I think. It was possible once. On a stay with my wife at the Yacht Club ten years ago, we could hear music being played next door on a gramophone. An attendant told us a man lived there – had done so, for years. Some sort of arrangement. I remember wondering what it would be like to lead his life – pure fantasy, of course, but I am a fantasist – and realizing that, with a few tweaks, it might be all right to be him. I never saw him. This is what's beautiful about staying in a club or hotel: you're invisible, as is your neighbour. Before that there was Bipul mama. He lived in Buckley Court. A bed and breakfast on Wodehouse Road. Even as a child I sensed that I would have gladly graduated to *being* him on the basis of the accommodation alone. Also the outhouse I could see from the twelfth-floor balcony in Malabar Hill. Unlike Buckley Court and Bipul mama, both gone now, it's still there. It met the criteria.

My talk's at four o'clock. 'A Critique of Specialization'. At one o'clock I must go to the top floor of a building behind Rhythm House to be in a Twitter 'chat' to promote the event. I end up wasting forty-five minutes 'chatting' with two organizers sitting next to me, talking rapidly to each other, and hiding behind their Twitter handles. I get up before the chat ends. They're a bit shocked by my abruptness. At half past three, I find one person in the library where I'm giving the talk: Ramu. We look for coffee. Collect two paper cups full of a sugary liquid and stand next to the statue of David Sassoon. It is as time-less and exquisite as a tree-trunk. He resembles an Arab prophet more than a Jewish merchant. People in Nehru jackets and jeans begin to gather. One or two finish a cigarette before they head to the garden. Resplendent, my chairperson walks in. I've never met her before. Her sari is simple and arresting, like a Rothko. At an un-specified moment, we exchange a nod and ascend the stage. She introduces me to the people in chairs, then leaves me. I expound with whatever ironical distance I can muster on my hatred of specialization. The audience is encircled by ferns. I think I spot Ramu. I'm not sure if that's him behind two women. He's in shadow. After the talk, he reappears – patient, like a family member at a wedding. I'm on a swift turnaround and have a panel discussion in an hour. The chairperson, her niece, Ramu, and I agree it would be best to pop across to Kala Ghoda for tea, notwithstanding the surge of humanity. We cross the street and plunge into the mad crowd and then materialize again in the narrow alleys near Trishna. We slip into a chic café-boulangerie, and, scouring the fur-niture for a free table, find Ramu's missing. Where is he? I look around me and step out on to the street. He's vanished, but I expect he'll turn up. I drink mint tea and we share a single muffin. Only in the evening do Ramu and I get to talk. 'I felt tired,' he says. There's no reproach in the voice, just sleepiness. Was he physically tired – or was it the company? Not that it matters. 'She's very beautiful,' he adds. 'Who?' 'The lady who was talking to you.' 'Which one?' 'Arrey, the one who spoke on the stage. *Really* beautiful. Speaks very well too.' I conjure her up. Already, the afternoon is long behind us. In Bombay, evening comes later than elsewhere, but it's so bright it annuls the day.

·◆·

My sliver of time is ending. In the morning, I check out. I entrust my small bag to the receptionist.

Ramu and I take a taxi to Malabar Hill. To get chutney sandwiches. I'll eat them on the flight. It's Ramu who reminds me. He offers to take me on the scooter. I refuse, and he accepts quietly. He would have insisted once. I think he should conserve his energy.

The Marine Drive's got the sun on its edges. Ramu's on my right, one arm straddling the back of the seat. I like it that he's invariably available – not just available; ready – for these excursions, right to when I leave for the airport. I worry about it too. I have a sense of leakage when I'm with him. Not just ageing – he's changed, I maybe less so – but a movement that was once an accumulation, a steady gathering, and is now leakage, a gradual seeping out of volume. I don't mean literally. He's gained weight, if anything. A couple of months ago, I asked him on the phone from Calcutta, 'So what are your plans for the day?' He paused for a second, then said, 'No plans. Just take it as it comes.' This is what I mean by leakage; this seeming stillness. Since his father died he's come into a very modest amount of money. I'm not sure how many years it'll last him. The 'factory' they had was sold off. For a year now he's been thinking of reinventing himself. A tourist guide for visitors to Bombay is what he'd like to be. 'None of these guides have any education,' he says, 'or my English.' It's true. Nor would they have his very particular vision of the city and its lanes and localities. This sensibility – of which he's only lately become aware – is what he wants to turn to his advantage, now he's back. But it isn't easy. He's too old to begin from scratch. He has an air of being established that belies his untestedness. Also, how long he could continue to live in Colaba is moot. He's been in that flat, which he shares now with an older sister, since he was a child. They pay rent. They'd get a substantial pagdi if they moved. Ramu's father used to periodically suggest they go to the outskirts and invest whatever remained. Though Ramu hated Colaba in those days, he strenuously resisted. It's the one wise decision he's taken.

I'm in luck. There are times when I reach the shop to find the chutney sandwiches gone, but not today. I buy four. They're so thin they might droop but for the butter gluing the slices together. I startle myself by paying for two chicken croquettes. Ramu demurs. If his father had been alive, he'd have felt the urge to get something. He has a traditional shopper's DNA, an eye for freshness and appearance.

Though we've left school behind, we keep returning to it. On the pretext of taking the arc round the club to Little Gibbs Road, we find ourselves moving in that direction. And, as we slow down instinctively, we discover the gothic building next to the Infant School is a church. Given it's *our* school (though we hated it), and despite not knowing the church's existence till this moment, we browbeat the watchman and ask to enter – though he doesn't need browbeating and would let us in anyway. We go inside in the manner of schoolboys. In school, the only time we had a sense of ownership was after hours, when we'd range across the empty classrooms with semi-savage ease. This is almost how we now explore the church, with the laxity of lapsed ownership. Not much to explore; it's tiny. Words that are alien to me but have been in my vocabulary since I was a child – pew, altar, chancel – come back vaguely to move me. Ramu is half Christian. He does go to church for funerals. But what holds us as we peer and poke around us is history. History is always lying before you, unnoticed: till you suddenly see it, as we do now.

*

'Okay, got to go.'

I'm suddenly mindful of departure. We have to have lunch – then I'll pick up my bag from the Astoria.

'What about Hanging Gardens?'

I shake my head. Our time here is done. I want us to dash into the National Gallery of Modern Art before I set out for the airport.

At half past two, I tell the driver of the limousine to pick me up from the NGMA. Odd, how they've put me up at the Astoria but given me a pick-up and drop-off in a white Mercedes. When it received me at the airport, there was a sign in the boot saying WELCOME USTAD AM-JAD ALI KHAN. The driver doesn't know where the NGMA is. 'Okay, you know Regal?' 'Yes, sir.' 'I'll be in front of Regal. We have to stop at the Astoria on the way.'

We cross at multiple lights before reaching the cinema. We lower ourselves on the steps. The February breeze is in my hair. I try to subdue it. A watchman orders all who are seated to vacate the steps. We rise obediently. Two European women take the watchman's directive with bad grace. We look towards Elphinstone College, at the steeples and grey and brown roofs. Dark dun-coloured buildings left behind at Independence.

'This is why I don't want to leave Colaba,' he confesses, forgetting how ferociously he used to resent it.

He's looking at the steeples dissolving into points with the eyes of one who thought he'd never be here. I feel sad too – not because of my departure, but because I can never tell when I'll see Bombay again. It's not that I'm going. *It* might.

•◆•

I see Bombay sooner than I'd expected. And Ramu. The reason is banal.

Barely a month's passed. My daughter's annual exams are done. My wife has one of her bouts of intense longing. She's keen to leave everything – 'everything' being Calcutta. 'Jaisalmer,' she says. For two decades, she's wanted to introduce me to Rajasthan – the forts, palaces, shrines; the brown horizons. But I'm resistant to history. I suppose I become unco-operative. 'Are you mad? Do you know how hot it will be?' I have no interest in the peacocks.

It turns out our daughter would tolerate going to Bombay. With its shops, cinemas, and cafés: Bombay, history's very antithesis. 'And clearly *you* don't need an excuse,' says my wife. She's at once resigned and invigorated. There's the prospect of much window-shopping. 'Tell you what,' I reply. 'Let's stay at the Taj – the old wing. I'll grovel and wheedle a special rate.' She stares at me. I don't splurge on hotels: they're taken care of by publishers and festivals. Holidays are combined with readings, a discounted package. And I've never stayed in the old wing. There was never a reason or opportunity.

I plead for a reduction. I do my best to impress the manager. 'You know, I wrote about the Taj for the *Guardian* the day after 26 November.' 'I see, sir,' he says with the requisite gravity. I go on, now shameless: 'Actually, a bit of my fifth novel describes the Taj.' Out of a sense of decency, he gives me a near-affordable rate for a sea-facing room.

The outing remains a secret. I don't tell my daughter. I want to surprise her. (My mother-in-law breaks it to her when they're together: 'I hear you'll be at the Taj.' My daughter forgets to mention this; so we don't know that she knows till I tell her later.) I hardly tell anyone in Bombay except Ramu. I don't want Janardhan to take over the visit. This is pure holiday. My wife and I resolve not to tell the wider world, because it might be best that people don't know we're staying in a fancy place. It's sure to be held against us.

By now, I'm well into a book. It's about Bombay. I've been writing it for a year.

I tell my wife: 'It isn't a holiday for me. It's a research trip.'

It's a well-known fact that no novel is taken seriously

in India until a good deal of research has gone into it. This stay in the Taj will be my research. Going down the stairs will be research. So will looking out at the sea.

In the meantime, because I'm writing, I'm thinking of Bombay. I think of Ramu. The Ramu I know and the Ramu I'm writing about have become indistinguishable. The same's true of the Bombay I'm recounting from experience and the Bombay I'm assembling through words. This is often how novels begin for me. There's a convergence. I live. Then something prompts me to write. The writing is not *about* life. It is a form of living. The two happen simultaneously.

I love the title, 'Friend of My Youth'. From an Alice Munro story. I haven't read the story. That's because the title must have implied a possibility. When that happens – when the title or first paragraph contains a promise – I become spellbound and keep returning to it. The work becomes irrelevant, the writer in me takes over from the reader, and my inchoate premonition of what the story will be dominates the story itself. I've hoarded titles and paragraphs for this reason, but never followed through. Naturally, when I first fell in love with Alice Munro's title, I had no idea that I'd one day want to write about Ramu and Bombay. Ramu was still to vanish. The experience of feeling unexpectedly bereft was to come. So were the attacks of 26 November. As these and other events happened, it's as if the title knew it had to meet them halfway; sensed it and they had been travelling towards each other.

The book is a novel. I'm pretty sure of that. What marks out a novel is this: the author and the narrator are not one. Even if, by coincidence, they share the same name. The narrator's views, thoughts, observations – essentially, the narrator's life – are his or her own. The narrator might be created by the author, but is a mystery to him. The provenance of his or her remarks and actions is never plain.

•◆•

We arrive in the afternoon.

This hotel, which I grew to avoid as a teenager, then saw nearly destroyed, holds a key to my memories. It's like 'the house of our life' that Benjamin mentions, with its 'perverse antiquities' – but not quite.

I collect three keys. They resemble old-fashioned keys, but the key-like bit is useless. It's the key ring that has the chip to the door.

There's an expectation, as you check in, that you might not go back – that you're about to be subsumed. A man escorts us to the room. These are passages you've only guessed at. Briefly passing a balcony, I see the in-tricate circuit of stairs reaching down from the third floor, where the room is.

I stare at the man's back as he taps key ring to lock.

There's a little hall at first, with wardrobe and storage space on the left. The bathroom is on the right.

Then comes the habitable part of the room, the bank of the bed, the table, chairs, and television, the pale win-dows. The paleness is the sea; as I approach the window,

I find the Gateway of India is at my left shoulder. Before me is the promenade, and water.

Ramu is a fifteen-minute walk away. I know he's at a loose end. Waiting for my call. I don't believe he's busy. My only concern is whether he's around – or gone. 'We're here,' I say. 'Ah, the prince of shaggers! Arrived from Calcutta, the intellectual capital!' 'What about you?' I say. 'Did I interrupt you while you were at it in the bathroom?' 'I'm still doing it,' he says with that sad tremolo. 'So when are you coming to the hotel?' He becomes lugubrious. 'You tell me. You should spend some time with your family, no?' 'No, no, they want to see you!' For my wife, Ramu's an inevitability. Or an anecdote from my childhood who's become inescapable. For my daughter, he's an atavistic apparition of whose meaning she's not sure. She first set eyes on him as an infant. I can't tell if she notices him – or any of us: she's so busy with her phone. 'Should I wait in the lobby?' 'Yeah, I don't think they'll let you up in the lift.'

In twenty minutes, there's a knock. I don't know how he managed to evade security. There he is, decently dressed, like a man on his way to the office.

Voices go high with hellos. He threatens my daughter, orders her to relinquish the phone. She grins at his forwardness.

'What a room!'

The fact that it exists is chastening. We become silent. We're at once watching and remembering.

'Look at this window!' I call him urgently.

'Why? Is it blood-spattered?'

'Just check out how old it is.'

I point to the neighbouring room. He ducks his head. The wood has lines where it could be riven, but is held together immovably. I last glimpsed such windows in Venice. Sometimes to look upon the old is not to discover the past: it is to see power.

•◆•

Breakfast is served at the Sea Lounge. We walk down two flights of stairs, stop at a gate that separates the first floor from the guests. A man in uniform unlocks it and lets us through. The gate is a memorial. It couldn't possibly bar people who'd decided to invade the upper floors. The pause we make before it opens is symbolic. In the Sea Lounge, Western and Indian breakfasts alike are steaming. Croissants, Danishes, crowd the plates. Not only is every detail restored – the food reminds you that nothing is stale or old: it's genuinely new. There's no question of going back. But the painstaking joining up of fragments is clear too. The vase is unbroken. And the bun is uneaten. I lift one with a tong.

I bargain persistently for a table by the window. I'm unsuccessful at first. But, from the second morning, the manager ensures good fortune for us. I don't know how he does it. My daughter and wife sit face to face. I drag a chair up and look at them and the sea.

•◆•

Cities are finite.

I haven't forgotten how Ramu – frequently 'slipping' in those days in 1986 – alerted me to the light smudge on the night sky where our galaxy seeps out. The sky was like a dark pane of glass we couldn't see through. It's because Ramu is used to looking out – from balconies; through windows – that we stood there and tried.

Ramu is where Bombay lives. I say this despite his not being well. The years of needle-jabbing were bound to have a consequence. His liver function's not right. 'I have a fantastic appetite, yaar!' he proclaims. He's *alive*.

He assesses my wife, my daughter, and me as a unit, without coming too close, checking to see if we're happy together and not malfunctioning. The trip has no literary distractions. I keep an eye on him. He's alive. Happiness comes later, if at all.

He wants to do my family a good turn.

'Can I bring them sweets? From Puranmal?'

'Don't. They're not interested.' My daughter's eating habits are bizarre and my wife hardly eats.

He stops, as if he'd been asked directions to a place and was trying to think of what to say.

He tells my wife slyly: 'Let me know if there's anything you want to see. I can take you on my scooter.'

It's his tourist-guide persona re-emerging, coupled with old romantic inclinations. He used to be popular with girls in school. In college, he shot off fast while they rode pillion. He never really reciprocated their feelings. Then he vanished for years, and only came into contact with women in his lucid periods as other people's wives.

She beams. Is she taking up his offer?

'Have you seen the Afghan Church?'

'Of course,' I say. 'In the military camp. I used to love the military camp.'

That was in 1980. We'd moved to Cuffe Parade. My father had become CEO. I hated Cuffe Parade and our four-bedroom apartment. The military camp was a short drive away, a pastoral created by the army and the navy. We went there to escape Cuffe Parade. Five minutes in, you saw the sole landmark, the Afghan Church.

'But have you been inside?'

Inside the church? The thought hasn't arisen. It

would be like entering a room whose door you never opened as a child.

My wife, come morning, wants to go to Contemporary Arts and Crafts at Kemps Corner – to see if it still exists. Ramu presses us to visit the church. We call an Uber. He sits in the front. The din of vendors opposite his building gradually gives way to Navy Nagar. (I can't explain why I've always called it 'military camp'.) Free movement is restricted here since 2008. The men with AK-47s alighted from dinghies at a fishermen's colony not far away. Almost comical, how they were confronted by, and rebuffed, the puzzled fisherfolk. But we can still access the church.

I love churches in Bombay. As a child, I conflated them with school; I felt disengaged from them. In 1985, I went twice with Ramu to a church in Mahim to attend NA meetings. In England, they never drew me: I thought they were dank. Now, they make me think of shadow. Of footfall on stone. In England, churches preside over their habitat till they're gratuitous. Here, they represent a journey made a hundred years or more ago. Our journey, before we go off to Contemporary Arts and Crafts, is brief.

We wander without purpose. Only my daughter is

preoccupied, trying to catch a signal. The doors are closed. Ramu spots someone shifty – a loiterer. He turns out to be the caretaker. He is bored. 'Come,' he says matter-of-factly. We think he wants money, but it turns out he's indifferent to a reward.

He lets us and the light in. The church is deeper and higher than I'd foreseen. At the far end are stained glass windows whose colours are apocalyptic and rainbow-like and miraculous.

I'd imagined the Afghan Church must be for Afghan Christians, whoever they might be. I'm unprepared for its actual meaning: it commemorates the English who fell in 1842 in Afghanistan. We peruse the names outside on a memorial stone. My wife, my daughter, and Ramu immediately gather round the memorial for a jovial photo opportunity. The fantasy generated by the environs is threatened momentarily. A photo is a record of being somewhere. Our excursion asks for no record. We don't want to know too much. Even about the church. Ramu and I skim impatiently over the information directed at tourists. He's never been able to read more than one page of a book at a time. Fantasists aren't natural readers. They grow restive easily.

•◆•

On the penultimate day we see each other at eleven, when my wife is attempting tentative swimming strokes, and my daughter is alone in the room with her phone. Parking his scooter in the lane that's at a right angle to the Taj, Ramu comes to the old entrance, which was closed a year ago but now has a small welcome party of security men. I wait here, out of the sun. We want to take a quick walk before my wife is ready to emerge. There's a tacit agreement between Ramu and me that I won't see him again. Nothing was said. No line has been drawn. We *might* see each other. But we won't. It's not I – *he'll* make excuses. He'll withdraw discreetly as I return to my family.

How many times we've gone down this promenade and lanes! For Ramu, the place became a curse – he's lived here without fully living life. No matter. No matter. Then, five years ago, he saw it was a blessing: being here. Once you move around the Taj, you become conscious of a series of dwellings and small hotels that haven't changed very much. Yet it's all changed.

Apollo Bunder is good for daydreaming. I used to come here when I was seventeen, eighteen, roam around the Gateway of India, and sit on the balustrade facing the Taj, never fully resting my bum because I was scared of falling into the sea. I would come alone. I did a lot of stuff alone – even went to movies by myself, which was a scandal. In Apollo Bunder, I'd watch people, and the water, and steamers returning. I felt a sharp need to be taken out of myself. This fancifulness became connected to my writing. I bought a blue exercise book and wrote the beginning of a story (I hardly wrote prose those days), about a man who came to Apollo Bunder, looked at the sea, to forget himself, to enter other lives. I made no advance on the beginning. Because the beginning made me rapt, and foreclosed development.

·◆·

I go with him. We turn right and right and keep going, passing his scooter. He nods at it, faintly patriarchal. At the lights, we stop and discuss where the Stiffles Hotel was.

A colonial house with a semi-haunted look. A bit like Norman Bates's home. Renowned in another age for hippies. Ramu points out an unprepossessing box-like hotel: 'That was Stiffles.' I shake my head in disagreement. Surely they wouldn't have destroyed it? The hotel next to the box resembles Stiffles, but has a different name. Its upkeep is excellent. We infiltrate the passage and open the door to reception. Here, we have a futile chat with a Fawlty Towers-type manager who's not in the least gratified by my interest. He keeps calling me 'My friend' and would clearly like us off the premises. He concedes tersely that the hotel next door came up where Stiffles was.

We're shocked by the hippies and the revolution they brought to Colaba. They lived partly in Stiffles and

155

partly on the footpath.

'I was with Hashim,' I say, thinking of this clean and empty spot as it was in 1976. Two Arabs sitting in front of an antiques shop greet me heartily. 'You know them?' asks Ramu. He's concerned that I might be enlarging my social life. 'No, people seem to recognize me here. I think they're reading my books. Yesterday,' I point to the street on the left, 'a drunk got up and shook my hand.' Ramu nods, grave. We swing round. The back of the Taj on our left. I'm very aware of my wife's proximity in the pool. I smile again at the Arabs. 'Anyway' – going back to 1976 – 'Hashim and I were walking and' – I gesture to an imaginary expanse in the shade – 'a woman was giving a man a hand-job over *there*.'

'Shit,' says Ramu, with an intake of breath at all the missed opportunities. 'Right in front of you?'

'Yes, yes, but under a blanket. We could see her hand moving. Actually, Hashim saw. I stepped on to the street.'

'Shit!'

Silence reigns as he immerses himself in the image. We walk. We are teenagers. We're more than fifty years old, but things that shocked us then shock us now. Family; fatherhood; unclehood (Ramu has two grown-up nieces); failure; near-death; the death of parents; the success of others – despite all this, the teenager is obstinate, and resurfaces at will.

'I liked Zohra Bandukwala,' he says. 'She liked me yaar.'

A forty-year-old extrapolation. They didn't know each other. She would have been aware of him as the gymnast and pugilist who wouldn't box or do gymnastics. Though she was short, she played basketball. Her socks collapsed to the top of her keds, her ankles glowed. He'd nudge me even then.

'You met her, no? What was that guy like?'

He's been consumed for three decades, through his ups and downs, with curiosity about her fiancé. Or the one who was her fiancé in 1985. His name escapes me. Satish, maybe. My father knew the fiancé's father. I didn't think I'd see Zohra that evening.

It hasn't occurred to me till this instant that it would have been an inter-religious marriage if they *had* married. But that's what the new Bombay does to your thinking. The fiancé's father lived in a flat facing the Oval Maidan. Probably costs twenty crores today. When I mentioned Ramu, her face went blank. Schoolgirl crushes are short-lived. I also suspect she was starting to realize she was bored of her fiancé. A good-looking, rich, boring young man. Kept encircling her waist with one arm – a tic – and she'd looked constrained. Yet she wouldn't have swapped him for Ramu. No, that would be stretching it, even in a romantic movie.

'He was stupid, kind of,' I say, as I've been claiming to him for thirty years.

He *was* stupid, kind of. The play-acting. The easy inheritance of his father's world. The silly at-homeness in the English language. Very Bombay. He would have eventually set poor Zohra's teeth on edge. The markets hadn't opened up then. He'd be fantastically rich now. Stockier. Far away from Oval Maidan. In the 'Bay area'. The words spoken in the same casual accent in which he said everything. He might be with Zohra. Or maybe he isn't. He's the sort of person you don't think of, but, if you do, sense the trajectory infallibly.

'I really liked Rani Rao.'

The stretch is residential. There's a park on our right. A few house staff dawdle on the footpath. The houses are a tropical mix of bungalow, art deco, and colonial. The lane leads to the T where Nigerian junkies, in the early eighties, furtively darted from one doorway to the other. We admire the poise of the houses. We know exactly where we are but imitate visitors who are lost.

Both us still refer to the girls in class by first and last name. Maybe because we didn't get to know them. Ramu's been loyal to his memory of Rani Rao. Zohra

Bandukwala had auburn eyes; Rani's were green. She had an imperfection which Ramu found endearing: she had a squint. She wore glasses with a thick black frame.

'She was sweet. But she was also tough.' He glances at me. 'No-nonsense. There was p-passion underneath.'

From time to time we stop beside the houses. We stand and look. The chiks half rolled up. The balconies partly concealing the living rooms. Foliage interfering with windows.

At which point we became aware of them I can't say. We sometimes talk more about houses than we do about girls.

I get a text. My wife is out of the pool. The phone begins to ring.

'Baba?'

'Yes – hi?'

'When are you coming back?'

'Ten minutes. Everything okay?' I speak to my daughter as if she's ten, not sixteen, years old. Like jet lag, this slow-moving childhood from which she's waking.

We reach the scooter. It's intact.

'You shouldn't have left Bombay.' He reprimands me while gazing abstractedly at the promenade. 'I don't have any friends left.'

I can't say the same. I *wanted* to leave. We stand before a boutique that used to be a nursing home. My childhood is trapped in these places. I can't take it away with me. I reacquaint myself with it when I return. The knowledge that I grew up here is an academic one. The insignificant particularities are lost, until I confront a street corner or sign or awning. Then I realize they're there for some reason, waiting for my return.

'I think you should shave that moustache off,' I tell him. I've just noticed it. Something wasn't right about him. Then I see it. A thin new moustache.

He's thunderstruck.

'Why?' One hand resting imperiously on the seat of the scooter.

'It makes you look like your father.'

I'd been thinking how he's become his father's twin. The resemblance, once I spotted it, was unnerving – the errant son giving birth to the solitary, aimless father. The son gone; only the father stays back in Colaba.

He ponders on my suggestion; lifts the scooter with a jerk.

'People say I look like him.' He's proud that his father was handsome. I can see that. I liked Ramu's looks. In college he'd blurt out with a hint of incredulity and self-congratulation: 'People say I look like Chunky Pandey yaar!' What happened to Chunky Pandey? He appeared in three or four movies; in a couple of years, he went into retirement. Then, in 1982, the year before I left for London, the year that followed *Rocky*, Ramu began to tell me, 'People say I look like S-sanjay Dutt!' I saw the likeness, though it's exceeded the physical by now. The time lost to drugs. The agony it brought the family, especially the fathers, who became minders. Dutt must have spent years in prison because of that stupid flirtation with the 1993 riots. Years. Years pass by in some people's lives. Astonishing stretches of time in which nothing happens except a suspension of fate. Yes, I saw the likeness. The bright eyes. The guileless- ness in the faces.

'It makes people take me more seriously,' he says of the thin moustache.

He kick-starts the scooter.

'It makes you look older.'

He's gone. His home is two minutes from here. Just be- fore Sassoon Dock. The Taj has been standing by. In- accessible, like a fortification. The 'house of our life'. Until the day after tomorrow. I go up to the promenade, turn, the sea behind me. I puzzle over the window of our room. They're hard to differentiate. Jutting out at angles, like the sides of a polyhedron. I call my daugh- ter. 'Come to the window. I'm standing below.' 'Where?'

'Right below. Dekhte pachho? In front of the water.' Nothing. Silence. Then: 'Yes.' I wave. I can't see her. 'Are you there?' I wave at a probable set of windows. 'Yes.' 'What are you doing?' 'I'm waving.'

It's even odder looking out of the hotel. From the Sea Lounge. Or the room. It's not just that you can't predict what you'll see. Each view has a history. You sense you're where others have been.

Often, I see people on the promenade looking up. Families from the provinces, three generations. Grandfather, grandchild, and whatever's in between. Europeans. They take aim with cameras. I'm reassured they can't actually see us. Even so, I feel I'm being speculated upon – as well as, for a moment, a dread that there's no way out of here.

I call Ramu in the afternoon. Already his voice sounds sluggish, as if I'd yanked him out of a well. 'Still shagging?' I enquire gravely. 'What else?' Then he asks: 'Achha, so what's happening this evening?' I don't tell him we're dining in, at the Lebanese restaurant on the rooftop. We've eaten once in the hotel. More than three meals will make a middle-class person poor. The Lebanese place has replaced the Rendezvous, where I used to go with my parents as a boy. You could see so much from the Rendezvous: even Bombay, which I thought of as dreary, appeared exciting in a cold, cinematic sweep. The lights, the office buildings, the tiled roofs far below, the dockyard, the exceptional dark of the water. I had to be impressed in spite of feeling bored. Rendezvous hovered above, yet was of, this world. So were we. I'd stare with reluctant affection at the outline of the building I lived in across the black expanse of nothing.

'Achha,' says Ramu, deliberating. 'You guys enjoy. I'm feeling tired. I'll chill out.'

'Hope to see you soon, sir.'

Checking out, I feel an urge to come back after specific intervals, to revisit the site of destruction – not of the hotel, which has for some time returned to completeness, but of the first part of my life.

'I hope so.'

'Thank you, sir. Did the concierge manage to get your wife the medicine?'

'He did.'

There's a loud voice coming from the first floor. I open the door to the stairs to take a look. A little group has congregated outside the Sea Lounge. Some of them I know by sight. A woman addresses them. 'Please follow me.' They vanish into an inner passage. I won't see them again. It's one of the hotel's new twice-daily heritage walks. We only just found out about them.

At the conclusion of Hollywood disaster movies and epics, time moves backward, piecing together like a jigsaw the elements that had come apart. The *Titanic* resumes its journey; Russell Crowe is reunited with his murdered wife and son. It's not a happy ending; it's a convention created for the purposes of an impossible sense of uplift at the end of death and tragedy: the happy beginning. Technology makes Hades unnecessary.

In the Taj, time moves both backward and forward. I check out; someone else has arrived. Suitcases follow in the bell boy's trolley. Nothing has changed. This is not an idyllic past that's been constituted again. It's the Taj as it is this afternoon; as it was on the afternoon of our arrival four days ago. We go to the lobby and wait for the Uber.

Acknowledgements

Thanks are due to –
those who have believed in my work and in this book:
Sarah Chalfant and Alba Ziegler-Bailey; Mitzi Angel;
Rajni George; and Sigrid Rausing, for also carrying an
excerpt in *Granta*.

A handful of friends I don't need to name.

As ever, my wife Rinka and my daughter Radha, who,
in different ways, make it possible for me to write.